Mara

WES
M

P9-DHH-089

THE LAST KIND WORDS SALOON

BY LARRY McMURTRY

CUSTER

THE BERRYBENDER NARRATIVES

HOLLYWOOD: A THIRD MEMOIR

LITERARY LIFE: A SECOND MEMOIR

RHINO RANCH

BOOKS: A MEMOIR

WHEN THE LIGHT GOES

TELEGRAPH DAYS

OH WHAT A SLAUGHTER

THE COLONEL AND LITTLE MISSIE

LOOP GROUP

FOLLY AND GLORY

BY SORROW'S RIVER

THE WANDERING HILL

SIN KILLER

SACAGAWEA'S NICKNAME:
ESSAYS ON THE AMERICAN WEST

PARADISE

BOONE'S LICK

ROADS

STILL WILD: SHORT FICTION OF THE AMERICAN WEST,
1950 TO THE PRESENT

WALTER BENJAMIN AT THE DAIRY QUEEN

DUANE'S DEPRESSED

CRAZY HORSE

COMANCHE MOON

THE
LAST KIND
WORDS
SALOON

⇒ A Novel ⇐

Larry
McMurtry

LIVERIGHT
PUBLISHING CORPORATION
A DIVISION OF W. W. NORTON & COMPANY
NEW YORK · LONDON

For information about permission to reproduce selections from this book,
write to Permissions, Liveright Publishing Corporation, a division of
W. W. Norton & Company, Inc., 500 Fifth Avenue, New York, NY 10110

For information about special discounts for bulk purchases, please contact
W. W. Norton Special Sales at specialsales@wwnorton.com or 800-233-4830

Manufacturing by Courier Westford
Book design by Lovedog Studio
Production manager: Anna Oler

Library of Congress Cataloging-in-Publication Data

McMurtry, Larry.
The Last Kind Words Saloon : a novel / Larry McMurtry. — First edition.
pages ; cm
ISBN 978-0-87140-786-3 (hardcover)
1. Earp, Wyatt, 1848-1929—Fiction. 2. Holliday, John Henry,
1851-1887—Fiction. 3. Western stories. I. Title.
PS3563.A319L367 2014
813'.54—dc23
2014002279

Liveright Publishing Corporation
500 Fifth Avenue, New York, N.Y. 10110
www.wwnorton.com

W. W. Norton & Company Ltd.
Castle House, 75/76 Wells Street, London W1T 3QT

2 3 4 5 6 7 8 9 0

For Susan Freudenheim,
a cherished friend.

THE LAST KIND WORDS SALOON
is a ballad in prose whose characters are afloat in time; their legends and their lives in history rarely match. I had the great director John Ford in mind when I wrote this book; he famously said that when you had to choose between history and legend, print the legend. And so I've done.

CONTENTS

THE LAST KIND WORDS SALOON

LONG GRASS

A hat came skipping down the main street of Long Grass, propelled only by the wind, which was sharp for March. The hat was brown felt and had a narrow brim.

"I believe that's Doc Featherston's hat," Wyatt said. "He may have lost track of it while setting a limb."

"Or, he might be over at the Orchid fornicating and let it blow out a window," Doc Holliday suggested.

"Doubt it . . . only rich dentists such as yourself can afford the Orchid these days," Wyatt said.

Doc drew his pistol and aimed at the hat but didn't shoot.

"Why would a grown man want to be a dentist anyway?" Wyatt inquired.

"Well, for one thing, the cost of equipment is low," Doc told him. "All you need is a pair of pliers and maybe a chisel for difficult cases."

At the mention of a chisel Wyatt turned pale—he had always been squeamish.

"I'm sorry I brought it up," he said. "Are we going to sit here and let the good doctor's hat blow clean away?"

A crow flew over. Doc shot at it twice, but missed.

Wyatt walked out in the street and picked up the hat.

Across the street, at the establishment called the Orchid a tall woman in a purple dressing gown came out onto a little balcony and shook out her abundant black hair.

"There's San Saba, what do you think about her?" Doc said.

"I don't often think about her," Wyatt said. "Jessie's all the female I can handle, and it ain't a hundred percent that I can handle her."

"Why do you ask?" he added.

"Just to be making conversation, I ain't a mute like you," Doc said. "And it's the only whorehouse in town. They say if you can sprout up twelve inches of dick you get to fuck free."

"Well, I can't sprout it up and I doubt you can so let's talk about something else," Wyatt suggested.

Just then they heard a faint sound from the empty plains to the south of town.

"There's supposed to be a herd coming in today from Texas—I 'spect that's it," Doc said. "Where's your six-shooter?"

"It might be behind the bar," Wyatt said. "It's too heavy to carry around. If I see trouble springing up I can usually borrow a weapon from Wells Fargo or somebody."

"Bat Masterson claims you're the best pistol shot in the West," Doc said. "He says you can hit a coyote at four hundred yards."

"Hell, I couldn't even see a dang coyote if it was that far away, unless they painted it red," Wyatt said. "Bat should let me do my own bragging, if he can't manage to be credible."

"All right then, what's the farthest distance you could hit a fat man?" Doc persisted, determined to get at least the elements of conversation out of the taciturn Wyatt, who ignored the question. In the distance it was just possible to see mounted figures, urging their horses at a dead run toward Long Grass.

"Those cowboys have probably been on the drive thirty or forty days," Doc said. "They're gonna want whiskey and whores, and want them quick."

Just then there was a piercing whistle, followed moments later by a train from the east; the train had many empty boxcars and two passenger cars and a caboose. As soon as it came to a complete stop a skinny young man got off, carrying a satchel.

"There stands a dude, of sorts," Doc said. "I wonder what the state of his molars might be."

"Now, Doc, don't be yanking teeth out of tourists," Wyatt said, turning pale again at the mere suggestion of dentistry.

The rumble to the south had diminished; for a time it faded altogether.

"The cattle smelled the water—they're over at the river, filling up," Doc said. "The whores can sleep a little longer."

"If you had twenty pearls would you give at least one or two to Jessie?" Doc inquired.

Wyatt ignored the question. His wife's taste for finery was none of Doc's business, that he could see.

One of the passenger cars was considerably fancier than the other. It was painted a royal purple. The skinny young dude took a moment to get his bearings and then came resolutely up the street.

"I wonder who's in that blue car," Doc said. "You don't often see a car that fancy in these parts."

He happened to glance to the south, where he saw two riders approaching. Wyatt noticed the same thing.

"Uh-oh," Doc said. "It's that damn Charlie Goodnight and his nigger."

"You're right—he was in that fracas in Mobetie," Wyatt said.

"They say that nigger is the best hand in the West at turning stampedes—it's a rare skill."

Just then Doc Featherston, owner of the bouncing bowler, walked out of the Orchid and fell flat on his face in the street.

"I guess San Saba likes the Doc," Wyatt said. "Women sure are odd."

Before Doc could weigh in on the oddity of women, San Saba herself walked out of the Orchid and strolled off toward the train track. The young man who had stepped off the train raised his hat to her. She took no notice of him, or of the prostrate doctor; nor did she so much as glance at the two men watching her from the porch of—according to its sign—The Last Kind Words Saloon. She went straight to the royal purple railroad car and rapped on the door, through which she was immediately admitted.

"Well, hell and damn," Doc said.

His taciturn companion said nothing at all.

· 2 ·

Charles Goodnight rarely troubled with pleas-
antries, but when he took note of the sign hanging over
the saloon door he stopped and gave the sign a considered
inspection.

"I wouldn't be surprised if one of my cowboys shoots a hole
in your sign," he said.

"When will that be, Charlie?" Wyatt asked.

"Soon as the herd's penned," Goodnight said.

"Ain't it a little early to be driving cattle on the plains?" Doc
said. "It's no fun driving cattle in a howling blizzard, which are
not uncommon in March."

"Driving cattle ain't fun, blizzard or no blizzard," Goodnight said. "But there's no train yet to my ranch, so here I am."

"Is that your sawbones sleeping in the street?" Goodnight
asked. "If it's who I think it is he once took a boil off my rump.
I've traveled more comfortably ever since."

"There's plenty of dentistry available here," Doc pointed out.

"Another time, maybe," Goodnight said. "I admire that sign, though I don't know what it means."

"It's my brother Warren's sign," Wyatt said. "I seldom understand Warren, myself."

While they talked, Bose Ikard, Goodnight's black foreman, saw a large bull snake edging around the porch. In his years on the plains Bose had learned a thing or two, one of which was how to catch snakes by the tail. He quickly caught the snake, swung him around his head a few times as if he were swinging a lariat, and threw him across the street, out of harm's way.

"He's just as neat with rattlesnakes," Goodnight volunteered.

"Bull snakes will charge you sometimes, and I am not a good enough shot to hit a charging snake."

"Me neither," Wyatt admitted. "I could probably hit a buffalo, though, if there were any left."

"We could stand here talking all day, which would not earn us a cent," Goodnight said. "Anybody get out of that blue railroad car?"

"No, but somebody went in it, the lovely San Saba," Doc said.

"Good, I believe I'll join the company," Goodnight said. He dismounted, handed his reins to Bose, who led his horse back toward the livery stable.

"How do you know you're invited, Charlie?" Wyatt asked.

Though he had no reason to be dismayed, he was dismayed.

Charlie Goodnight, in an excellent mood, was strolling down the street to join the most beautiful whore on the plains, and somebody rich enough to travel in a fancy railroad car. Private cars in royal purple or just plain blue didn't show up in Long Grass every day.

"Hell and damn," Doc repeated. He was puzzled too.

·3·

"Charlie Goodnight's known to be irascible," Wyatt said, to Doc. "It's rare that he's even polite."

"What did you say he was?" Doc asked.

"Irascible, clean out your damn ears," Wyatt said.

"It's too much word for me, that's all," Doc protested. "Some days you just talk funny."

"Look, Charlie's got Doc Featherston on his feet," Wyatt said. "No doubt Charlie's grateful—for a man in the saddle as much as he is, a boil on the rump would be vexatious."

"I expect this dude is a cattle buyer," Doc said. "Charlie didn't drive his cattle all the way up here just to park them in a pen."

Goodnight ignored the dude with the satchel and walked up and rapped on the door of the fancy railroad car, which opened immediately. A tall figure shook Goodnight's hand vigorously and rapidly pulled him in.

Wyatt and Doc caught a glimpse of San Saba before the door closed.

"Today's off to a peculiar start, I'd say," Wyatt said.

Before Doc could answer, the dude with the satchel came in hearing distance.

"Good morning, gentlemen," the skinny young man said. "Could you direct me to the newspaper office? I'm a reporter, you see."

"Or if there's a boardinghouse nearby I might go there first and secure a room."

"I'm Billy Pippin," he added.

"Before you go to the trouble we best figure out if you're in the right town," Wyatt said. "This is Long Grass, which is nearly in Kansas, but not quite. It's nearly in New Mexico, too, but not quite. Some have even suggested that we might be in Texas."

"It depends on your notion of where Texas stops," Doc said, for clarity's sake.

By which point young Billy Pippin looked thoroughly confused.

"The one thing that's certain is that Long Grass has no newspaper office," Wyatt said.

"For that matter it has no news," Wyatt told him. "Very little happens here, son."

"But it will have some: Goodnight and Lord Ernle are about to partner up and have the biggest ranch in the world. I work for the *Chicago Tribune*. I'm expected to file a story. I need a telegraph."

"Oh, if that's all you want there's one right over in Rita Blanca, if you can put up with the woman who runs it— I can't," Wyatt said.

"Miss Courtright, why she's the very one who encouraged me to come," Billy Pippin said.

"Nellie Courtright could peel paint off a fence, just by talking," Doc said.

Billy Pippin looked defeated.

"How far is Rita Blanca?" he asked.

"Too far to walk," Wyatt said. "But there's buggies for hire if you're rich."

"No, no, I'm not rich," Billy objected. "I'm just trying to file a story about this merger—the English lord and the Texas rancher, you know."

Just then, to their surprise, San Saba stepped out of the railroad car. Four pigeons perched on her arm. One by one she held them up and released them. Two flew east and two flew south.

"They're messenger pigeons, I'm scooped for sure," Billy Pippin said. "Lord Ernle really means to get the news out."

"News from pigeons! Where will the damned birds go?" Doc asked.

"One to Kansas City and probably one to Fort Worth," Billy said.

"Hawks might get one—'spect why he sent out two," Bose said.

"I've never supposed a damn pigeon could find its way to Fort Worth, and I ain't convinced it will," Wyatt said.

"Besides that, how does San Saba get to know a lord?" Doc asked. The migrations of beautiful women had always interested him.

"He bought her from a sultan—they say she's a virgin," Billy Pippin said. "My bosses want to know if it's true."

"A what?" Doc said, thinking he must have heard wrong. How many virgins spent their time running whorehouses on the plains?

Before they could discuss it further there was a rumble from the south.

"The cattle got penned, cowboys are coming," Bose said.

Wyatt moved quickly for the first time.

"I need to wake up my wife, she's the best bartender in Long Grass," he said.

"Save me a toddy," Doc said, but by then Wyatt was long gone, into the Last Kind Words Saloon.

· 4 ·

"You just made me a bartender so you could keep track of me in the afternoon . . . the slack time."

"And the morning, and around midnight," Wyatt said.

"Besides, a little education don't hurt," he added.

"Bartender's school in Kansas City ain't exactly education," Jessie pointed out. It irritated her that her husband was so hard to talk to. Three or four complaints in a row and he'd usually slap her, and once or twice he'd done worse, which is why she was careful to keep the bar between them most of the time. He wasn't tall enough to reach her all the way across the bar, but she knew he had it in him to hit her hard.

Twice when she had pushed him over the limit—which she did mainly to find out what his limit was—he had hit with his closed fist and knocked her sprawling. It took talent to make Wyatt lose his temper, but Jessie knew just how to do it, and did it mainly just to have something happening. Pouring whiskey from bottle to glass was boring work. Needling Wyatt was the way to start something; or would have been if Wyatt ever took the trouble to make up with her. Then she might have taken him in hand and gotten him active, but only if she was quick to take him in hand; otherwise he'd go to another saloon and get drunk—after which she might not see him for days.

Wyatt had a big reputation as a gunfighter, which puzzled Jessie, because as far as she knew he had never actually killed anybody. When she asked him about it he said that he had never needed to, and perhaps never would.

But Jessie had no doubt that Wyatt would kill somebody, someday, for something or for nothing. There was something hard in Wyatt that wasn't in his brother Morgan or his brother Virgil, though they were actually lawmen for real, Morgan usually a sheriff and Virg usually a deputy. But whoever was the official marshal, Wyatt was the real law, even though he had never officially been hired, much less elected.

"Vote for Wyatt, no," Doc said, when Jessie pinned him down about the matter. "Only a fool would vote for Wyatt."

"But they'd vote for you, wouldn't they?" she asked. Jessie liked Doc, although she knew he was rarely sober.

"If I cared to charm them, yes," Doc said. "But there's no place I'd care to be elected at, so it's back to the cards. Wyatt thinks I'm the best poker player in America. Jessie, what do you think?"

Jessie liked to keep Doc talking, in case he might accidentally touch her or something, and if they ever accidentally touched in the right place, then he'd be hers, Wyatt or no Wyatt.

"You ain't afraid of Wyatt, are you, Doc?" Jessie asked.

"Jessie, I don't give enough of a damn to be afraid of any-thing," Doc said, and he looked as if he might know what she was thinking.

Then he laughed.

"Women, women, women," he said. "Why are you thinking of doing the one thing that might make Wyatt Earp kill you?"

"To see if he's alive," she said. "To see if he cares."

"And you can't figure that out without risking gunplay?"

"I haven't so far," Jessie said.

"When I try to talk to Wyatt he just walks out and the next thing I know he's down the street, drunk, with that little shot-gun of his."

"It's his weapon of choice," Doc said. "It's ideal for whack-ing noisy cowboys in the noggin so they can be drug off to jail. Wyatt usually does the whacking and leaves the dragging for Virgil."

"You're not being a lot of help, you know," Jessie said. But Doc just sat there staring into space until Jessie thought to hell with it and walked away.

· 5 ·

"I was raised by the eunuchs," San Saba said. "There were fifty in the seraglio, Mr. Goodnight."

The two of them were watching Lord Ernle enjoying a foot-bath.

"Very important to keep the feet clean," he went on. "Many infectious evils come in through the soles of the feet."

"Fifty eunuchs?" Goodnight said; the morning was rich in surprises.

"My mother was the Rose Concubine, which was a very high position in the harem. But one day she refused the sultan, which was not done."

Goodnight waited.

"He had her blinded, sewn in a sack, and thrown off a cliff into the Bosphorus. I was kept a virgin until the sultan got around to me. Fortunately Benny showed up and bought me."

"Rather filthy specimen, that sultan," Lord Ernle said. "Hamid something. I couldn't see wasting such beauty on Orientals. But that's a long story and I think Charlie and I ought to be thinking about our announcement."

"Okay," Goodnight said. "There's a newspaperman wandering around here already and there'll soon be a passel more. I'm sure Nellie Courtright will soon be along—she runs the telegraph in Rita Blanca, which ain't far—at least not as the crow flies."

He was trying to learn a new virtue: patience. He was known all over the West for exactly the opposite quality: impatience; and, in his impatience, he was known to be exceedingly profane—and loud to boot. His own wife, Mary Goodnight, had threatened to leave him twice because of the cussing, although in neither case was it her he was cussing.

Though impatient, Goodnight wasn't daft. He had met Lord Ernle in Chicago, where an effort was made, although a feeble one, to form a stockmen's association, and he liked Lord Benny Ernle immediately, while recognizing that he wasn't an ordinary partner. He was the tallest man in England, and also the richest: one of his many country houses, he told Goodnight, required thirty-eight gardeners.

"Weeds, I suppose," Goodnight said, but Lord Ernle didn't hear him. He was left to wonder what thirty-eight gardeners did. Though he had known Lord Ernle only a few months he realized that he would be wasting his time trying to understand English ways; maybe his wife would have better luck when they met up, as they would soon.

"What's the word on my house? San Saba and I are looking forward to moving in soon," Lord Ernle said.

Even before the partnership with Goodnight had fully evolved, Lord Ernle had made himself a legend in the West by ordering the construction of a vast castle on a bluff overlooking the Canadian River. Miles of train track had been laid just to bring workmen and equipment to the castle site. Though still a vast shell, travelers who happened on it were left speechless by the scale. Even Mary Goodnight had been struck speechless, a rare occurrence in Charlie's experience.

"I fear I had no time for architecture," Goodnight said. "But I did bring up about fifteen hundred yearlings for us to put in play."

"Not to worry, Mr. Goodnight," San Saba said. "We left a foreman there to see that construction is moving along. I even have photographs. There's a lot to do yet but it'll get done in time."

"I rarely do worry," Goodnight said, while wondering exactly what role San Saba—once maybe the most beautiful woman in Asia, now no longer in Asia—would have in this hastily evolved partnership. Though gossiped about endlessly in the cow country, not much was actually known about her. She called Lord Ernle Benny, but what did that mean? There was said to be measuring of penises at the Orchid, but was it true and if so what did *that* mean?

"What about the savages, Charlie?" Lord Ernle inquired. "All subdued, I trust?"

Goodnight shook his head.

"The Comanches are through—they've accepted reservation life," he said. "With the Kiowa it's a shakier situation. There are twenty or thirty renegades who keep breaking loose and causing trouble."

"Why not raise a private militia and go wipe the devils out?" Lord Ernle said. "I'm sure there are plenty of fine killers for hire in these parts."

"Yes, but most of them are worse than the Kiowa," Goodnight said.

"The Texas Rangers are trying to corral them, but they're sly rascals," Goodnight said. "There are lots of pistoleros we could get but they are a mixed blessing, Ben."

"Will Mrs. Goodnight be visiting us at the castle?" San Saba asked. "I'm anxious to meet her."

"She'll show up, I can't say when," Goodnight said, remembering a sharp little exchange he had with his wife as he was leaving to gather the herd. He had suggested that they live in a tent for a while, until he could build them a house of their own.

"You want me to live in a tent?" Mary said, with an unfriendly cast to her expression. "Your partner and his concubine live in a fine mansion while I live in a tent? How is that fair, Charlie?"

"I doubt she's his concubine," he said. "And I'll get us a house started as soon as I get the money from this cattle sale."

"I didn't learn algebra just to live in a tent," Mary said—a remark that puzzled him a good deal, since Mary had never so far burst into algebra. Where did she learn it, and why?

The question was amenable to no immediate answer, since Mary Goodnight turned and walked away.

· 6 ·

"There's seven of them," Satank said. "I don't think they all have guns. We can catch them and burn them right now."

"They might have rifles in the wagons, where we can't see them," Satanta, the Red Bear, pointed out.

They watched from a little copse of trees near the Wichita River as a small party of teamsters, in three wagons, struggled over the rocky ground. Earlier that day some soldiers came by, too many to challenge—though Satanta, who was reckless to the point of folly, wanted to challenge them anyway. But Satank and Little Wolf persuaded the warriors to wait for easier prey— maybe there would be some women they could rape and torment.

When the seven teamsters came into view Satank was disappointed that no women were with them, but seven white men were better than nothing.

The teamsters were using oxen, rather than mules, which made them easier to catch, but, even so, one white man got away into the chaparral. That left six, and two of them put up such a stiff fight that it was necessary to kill them directly, rather than with torture. Of course they castrated and scalped them anyway, although they weren't alive to feel it.

That left four teamsters and they each paid a heavy price for having blundered into the People's country. The leader, a stout man who yelled the loudest, was chained facedown from a wagon tongue and slowly burned alive—his screams could be heard for a long time, along with those of a tall boy who had his genitals cooked over a small fire that Satank himself had carefully nursed along.

The other two teamsters were disemboweled, their guts pulled out so some hot coals could be stuffed into their stomach cavity. Satank also cut off their noses and forced them to eat some of their own offal.

Afterwards the members of the little war party felt fine. Torturing whites was a splendid way to spend the afternoon. Seeing to it that your enemies died as painfully as possible was the best revenge for what the whites had taken from them. It was a little disappointing that no women had been caught. Women's breasts could be cut off or their privacies invaded with thorns or scorpions or hot coals; but sometimes they could only catch men.

Satanta rubbed some of the red clay with which he covered his body on the corpses of the dead men. "I want everybody to know it was me that killed them," he said.

"Don't be bragging, you fool," Little Wolf said.

"He always brags," Satank reminded them. "We all killed them together, but he wants the whites to think it was only him."

"It was mostly me," Satanta protested.

The others decided to leave. Satanta, the Red Bear, was often difficult. It was best to leave him alone and savor the happy day a little.

· 7 ·

San Saba wore a big floppy hat out to the cattle count, which took place early in the day, by the ramp up which the cattle were crowded into the boxcars. She had a pad in her hand and sat on a high chair provided by the railroad.

Goodnight was startled to see the tall woman preparing to count cattle, but not as startled as Brownie, his horse, by the big floppy hat.

To Goodnight's embarrassment Brownie began to crow-hop, something he had not done in years. He soon brought him under control.

San Saba secured her hat with a drawstring.

"At home in Derbyshire I mainly count sheep, but Lord Ernle thinks I'll do fine with cattle."

Goodnight could think of nothing to say, so he said nothing and nodded to Bose. Soon cattle began to surge up the ramp, into the waiting boxcars.

Goodnight prided himself on his ability to count cattle. What it took was concentration, and he could concentrate when it was called for.

San Saba occasionally made a mark on her pad. Some cattle were reluctant to load and had to be quirted.

"I measure them in tens, which seems prudent," she said. When the loading was complete she showed Goodnight the total on her pad: 1,266, exactly the total. Goodnight had arrived at the same number by the use of his two eyes.

"I confess I'm surprised. I had not expected the two of us to have exactly the same count," Goodnight said. "You're a fine counter. Very few cattle men can count yearlings on the hoof."

"I concentrate," she said. "But I write down numbers. I didn't see you write anything down."

"What bothers me, ma'am, is that Lord Ernle must not have trusted my count. If Ben ain't going to trust me, then this partnership ain't like to work."

San Saba gave him a long look.

"He trusts you, Mr. Goodnight. But the English are different, and they don't know how to be other than different. Particularly not dukes."

"Did he really give you a diamond, back in Turkey or wherever you were?"

"Yes, the San Soucis diamond, it's very famous."

Then she turned and walked off. Mary had turned and walked off. He wondered what prompted females to keep showing him their rumps.

· 8 ·

The sun was blazing hot and Wyatt and Doc had just settled down on the porch of the Last Kind Words Saloon when they saw a buggy coming from the east—and coming at a furious pace, too. Doc was savoring an early morning brandy, while Wyatt was drinking black coffee and trying to sober up. He had slept in the stables most of the night, driven out by Jessie's sharp tongue. Lately she had seemed to find life with him most disagreeable. He didn't know why.

"That buggy's practically flying," Doc observed. "Why would anyone be in that big a hurry to arrive in no more of a town than this?"

"Maybe it's the Pony Express," Wyatt said. Often he wished Doc would just shut up.

"Nope, the Pony Express is out of business," Doc announced cheerfully—"it was a darn slow way to get mail, anyway, if you ask me."

"I hope the dern buggy plans to pass on through," Wyatt said. "It's crowded enough here already."

"Crowded? Not that I notice," Doc said.

The buggy slowed as it passed the livery stable and finally pulled to a stop right in front of them. The dust of its passing took a while to settle.

A tall man wearing a long coat and a soft felt hat extracted himself from the buggy and looked the two of them over before committing himself to speech.

"Does this settlement have a name, gentlemen?" he finally asked, as he handed some bills to the man who drove the buggy.

"Most of us call it Long Grass," Doc said. He had an impulse to shoot the man, but managed to hold off—sometimes he couldn't manage restraint, in which case his victims often required medical care. He decided not to shoot the tall stranger, mainly because he admired his soft felt hat.

The stranger managed to heave a well-worn satchel out of the buggy before it left—which was immediately. The satchel looked heavy.

"What's in that valise, ingots?" Doc asked.

"Everything I own, which doesn't include many precious metals. I'm Russell of the *Times*."

He seemed to think they would know what he meant, but neither of them bothered to look up. Surprised, the man then took out two business cards and handed one to each of them.

"Which *Times* are you of, Russell?" Doc asked, as Wyatt stared rather dubiously at the card he had been handed.

"Fine print, can't read it," Wyatt said. He tried to hand the card back to the stranger, but the stranger declined to take it.

"London, sir—the *Times* of London," Russell said.

He seemed a little vexed, Doc didn't know why. He and Wyatt could not be expected to know the identity of every fool that rides up.

Now the stranger was looking closely at the sign, a normal enough sign, Doc felt, though the only important word on it was "saloon." The rest was the sort of nonsense that interested Warren Earp.

"I was told about your sign, and there it is," Russell said. "Myself, I rarely frequent barrooms if I'm hoping for kind words."

"That driver of yours looked familiar," Doc said. "But I can't call his name."

"Willy Bones, once a trapper on the Missouri," Russell said. "I fear prospects are thin for trappers now."

Neither Doc nor Wyatt had any interest in trappers, so they held their peace, as the tall reporter gave Long Grass a thorough looking-over.

"Would the cattle on that train belong to Lord Ernle, by any chance?" he asked.

"Charlie Goodnight brought those cattle here," Doc said. "I believe his partner is an English fellow—he might be your lord, and he might be in that fancy car, unless he's in the whorehouse."

The stranger emitted a guffaw.

"Lord Ernle has two wives, one French and one English," he said. "You must understand they leave him little time for whoring. How far away would you reckon Arizona to be?"

"Why, Arizona's to hell and gone," Wyatt said. He felt like he might be ready for a whiskey.

"It's two or three states to the west," Doc said. "I wouldn't attempt it in that buggy."

"I hadn't planned to," Russell said. "I might catch this train here to Chicago, where these cattle are bound. From Chicago I ought to have a chance of reaching Arizona."

"Well, but there's Apaches," Doc said. "It would be a pity if you got scalped."

The Englishman's cool tone irritated him. Why would someone from London show up in Long Grass if Arizona was where he really wanted to go? The last twenty-four hours had produced more surprises than were welcome, he considered.

Across the way, on the balcony of the Orchid, two young whores stood with San Saba, just looking around. A young whore whose name was Flo was combing out San Saba's abundant black hair. San Saba herself was looking at nothing; and certainly, on the vast windy plain, there was plenty of nothing to be looked at.

· 9 ·

The village of Long Grass, which some thought to be in Texas, was suddenly startled by a high-pitched squealing, so taxing to the ear that most citizens assumed that massacre was at hand, or had already happened. Wyatt, who had been drinking in the livery stable, came running out with a pitchfork, the only weapon he could lay a hand on quickly.

But, once in the street, he saw no Indians to stick a pitchfork in.

Doc's predicament was even worse: he had won considerable money at poker during the night, and was standing on the porch, with most of the money in his hand, when the squealing started. The terrible sound confused him so that he dropped the bills, which were at once picked up by the brisk prairie wind and blown every which way.

"Goddamn the goddamn Indians!" he exclaimed, though for

some reason he could see no Indians as he continued to chase his money, catching a bill here and there but letting two get past him for every one he caught. He had his pistol in his right hand and had to grab at the blowing bills with his left, which was not ideal by any means.

Goodnight had a small house arranged for him by Lord Ernle—he was dozing when the squealing started; in jerking awake he bumped his head on a shelf he hadn't noticed. He had merely used the house as a place to trim his beard. He preferred to sleep outside unless it was wet.

The only people not bothered by the squealing were San Saba, and Russell of the *Times*; these two citizens of the world had encountered one another, over the years, here and there, in places no less prepossessing than Long Grass.

"It's just Benny's bagpipes," San Saba said, as Flo, the Creole girl, arranged her hair, watched by Russell of the *Times*.

"Dreadful sound, except to the Scottish ear," he said. "I don't happen to have a Scottish ear."

"At least the cattle left," San Saba said. "What a stench! There was a train that came in late, which probably accounts for the bagpipers, and a good many more reporters. Uncle Benny does love publicity: he wants the world to know he's setting up to be a cowboy."

"Rather late in the day to be starting up a ranch," Russell said. "Them blizzards cost the cattlemen fifty million in frozen stock. Taught most of them a lesson."

San Saba fell silent. Lord Ernle was so rich that it had never occurred to her that any enterprise of his might fail. And yet her own experience should have made her skeptical. Her own mother had been the most pampered woman in Turkey, and yet she was sewn in a sack and drowned.

"He's taken a very able partner, at least," she said. "I believe Mr. Goodnight will protect him well."

"Yes, he was once a Texas Ranger, I believe—they have to be able if they hope to survive," Russell said. "I endeavor to draw him out about frontier conditions, if I can get him to sit for an interview."

San Saba liked it that Goodnight had complimented her fairly for her accurate count; still there might be something in him that was too hard, that probably wouldn't tolerate the feminine element to any serious degree.

And yet a woman, Mary Goodnight, had not only married him: she had followed him into the wilderness, where San Saba hoped to meet her. Now, San Saba wondered, could any woman live every day with that level of masculinity?

It certainly wasn't there in Benny Ernle, who ignored his two wives while enjoying his many boys.

"I think the frontier is safe now," she said; but the reporter shook his head.

"Nope, there's just been a massacre," Russell said. "I picked it off the wire before I came. Some Kiowa did it, they think. The usual tortures, six teamsters butchered and burnt. General Sherman was nearby and he's pursuing."

"I remember Mr. Goodnight mentioning some Kiowa. Benny says he knows the West better than any man since Kit Carson."

"I interviewed Kit Carson twice, but now he's dead," Russell said.

"Perhaps Mr. Goodnight will do just as well. Benny says he's never been lost, night or day, in any weather."

Russell had been sitting; he stood.

"If I may say so, Miss San Saba, you're just as beautiful as ever."

San Saba didn't answer. She was thinking of Mr. Goodnight. Why, she couldn't say.

"Satank," Goodnight said at once, when the tall Englishman told him about the massacre. "The son of a bitch, he's the worst Indian still out. Although Satanta ain't far behind. Satanta tried to hug me once, but since he smears himself with red clay I declined the hug."

"He was there too," Russell said. "And several others whose names I didn't recognize."

"If you got Satank and Satanta you're damn well informed, for a person from as far away as London."

"Yes, that's what we English do now: we stay informed," Russell said.

"And invest," Goodnight added. "If it wasn't for Lord Ernle's investment I wouldn't be here flapping my jaw with a scribbler like you."

Goodnight was restive: the minute he heard about the mas-

sacre he wanted to get home to Mary. But he was trapped. Lord
Ernle, his partner, was bringing in three special train cars full
of dignitaries. At least three governors were there, plus big
lawyers and bankers, a few millionaires, and, of course, many
journalists. Benny Ernle had to be allowed his party. While the
townsfolk and cowboys looked on in amazement, a huge tent
was erected, champagne popped, a beef was roasted, chilled
pheasants were brought in from Virginia, a thousand quail's
eggs were served up as appetizers, and nearly everybody got
drunk.

"I didn't even know a damn quail could lay an egg," Wyatt
declared. He himself had been interviewed several times, and
Doc too. Wyatt was hailed as hero of Abilene and Dodge, but
he had little interest in compliments, unless they came from Jessie, which lately they didn't.

"Why me?" Wyatt asked, when told he was a hero of some
sort. "Abilene and Dodge are just as mean and ugly as they
were before I went there. I subdued a few cowboys who had
drunk too much for their own good, that's all."

"You're an anomaly, sir," Russell told him. "Most lawmen I
know take a little more in their own reputations."

Wyatt shrugged and walked away. Charlie Goodnight's
noisy party didn't interest him. He thought he might rope one
or two of the bagpipers, but never got around to it.

"I wish Charlie Goodnight had put his ranch somewhere
else," Doc said. "I've talked so much I'm hoarse."

"The ranch *is* somewhere else," Wyatt explained. "This is
just his shipping station."

"That tall English reporter is going to Arizona," Doc said. "Maybe we ought to tag along."

In fact Wyatt had been thinking about a move. He found that he soon tired of most places on the plains: the same drinking, the same card playing, the same rough society; not to mention Jessie's variable moods. She had never liked the plains. Arizona, he understood, was mostly desert. Maybe she'd like the desert better. But, short of moving to it, how to know?

Meanwhile, in the main street of Long Grass a whole beef had been roasted, and a large black butcher was carving it up and handing hefty slabs to cowboys and dignitaries alike. One hundred pheasants from Virginia were fast consumed. Doc Holliday, a stranger to quail's eggs until that day, liked them so much that he ate forty. A veritable river of drink was imbibed. Food disappeared so quickly that a second beef was roasted, from which Lord Ernle himself cooked the sweetbreads.

While the vast company was feasting a tall man came riding in on a white horse: Buffalo Bill himself, accompanied by his longtime chum—some said mistress—Nellie Courtright, the tall telegraph operator from nearby Rita Blanca.

Goodnight had long admired Nellie Courtright, a woman with spunk if there ever was one. Once or twice he considered proposing to her; but one day he came back from a cattle drive only to discover that Nellie was married and already pregnant—which she was often in the next few years, in one of which Mary Anne came along and proposed to him.

"I thought the man was supposed to do the asking," he said, though in mild tones.

"You're living in the past, Charlie," Mary Anne said, and that was that.

Nellie, spunkier than ever, marched right in and handed a telegram to Lord Ernle.

"Don't lose it, it's from the president himself," she said.

"Well, I won't," Lord Ernle assured her. He was often taken aback by forthright women.

Goodnight thought that Cody seemed tired. He was showman enough to manage a fine entrance, but his face was gaunt; and he was not slapping backs and hurrahing with the dignitaries, as he once would have.

"He's failing, my Billy," Nellie said. "And he's no longer his own man. A newspaperman in Denver owns him lock, stock, and barrel."

"Harry Tammen, the son of a bitch," Goodnight said. "He don't own me, but he's done me some bad turns."

"He is a son of a bitch," Nellie said. "I can't afford to go to jail—who'd look after my girls—but if I could I'd shoot him for what he's done to Bill Cody."

·11·

Goodnight was startled by Nellie's cussing. He had never heard the term son of a bitch employed by a female. He coughed to hide his embarrassment, but he needn't have, because Nellie was heading over to chat with Doc Holliday, who was thinking that he might have overdone the quail's eggs.

"Where's Wyatt?" Nellie asked.

"He seen you coming and hid," Doc said. It was hardly even a lie. "I'm not so quick on the uptake, or else I'd be hid too," he told her bluntly.

"You two could be nicer to me—it wouldn't require much effort. Because like me or not I'm here to stay."

She sighed. Men were a pain.

"When Wyatt comes out of hiding, tell him I need to ask him something," she said.

"It might be next week," Doc said, improvising.

"No it won't, unless Jessie has finally left him. What's the odds on that?" she asked.

Before Doc answered Nellie observed that Lord Ernle was making toasts—and she wanted to listen. The English were good with toasts. She listened to a few and had to admit that Lord Ernle made splendid use of the English tongue. He toasted the president, and the governors and his new partner Goodnight, and the cook and the newspapermen and plenty of others. Nellie half expected to be toasted herself, but she wasn't, and neither was San Saba, who was watching the proceedings quietly, along with Flo, the Creole girl who did her hair. Later in the afternoon Nellie spotted San Saba going into the Orchid, a hotel known to be a whorehouse, and followed her.

"San Saba, I'm Nellie—could I take a few minutes of your time?" she asked.

San Saba turned at once.

"Let me ask the first question—is Mr. Cody really your lover?" she asked.

"Nope," Nellie said. "I've never been his mistress, although there's been just a little kissing and some other stuff."

"What other stuff?"

"He likes to feel my titties—he's harmless now."

"Well, I'd say Mr. Cody is lucky to have such a considerate friend."

"Excuse me, but since we're on the subject, are you Lord Ernle's mistress?"

She was afraid she might never have a better chance to ask

that question, and she wasn't going to succeed in newspapers if she didn't ask the big questions when she could.

"No, I'm merely his best madam," said San Saba. "And to some extent his foreman. Benny Ernle saved me, schooled me, trained me, but then look where he put me? I deserve New York, Paris, Bombay, don't you think, Miss Courtright?"

"You sure do," Nellie said, wondering what she would find out next.

"He stuck me here because he's afraid to risk putting me in one of the capitals," San Saba said.

"Why?"

"He's afraid someone richer might snatch me. Now he's sending me off to Texas with your cattle, so I won't run off."

"Good god," Nellie said. "I didn't think anybody was rich as Lord Ernle."

"There's a few challengers," San Saba told her. "Maharajahs and such."

"You're probably the most interesting woman I've ever met," Nellie said. "I wish you'd let me do a magazine piece on you."

"Not a chance," San Saba told her. "I'm a madam, remember—I have to be discreet. But I will invite you to visit us in our Texas house, when it's complete."

They stood for a minute, with Flo, the Creole girl, standing just behind San Saba.

"That's an interesting sign for someone who wants to be discreet. Do you really measure customers?"

"Flo usually measures them, when there's some question of length. Though I am familiar with the procedure," San Saba said.

Nellie could not imagine doing something like that with her husband Zenas. He would no doubt accuse her of not doing him justice, though she felt a little dewy between the legs just at the thought. Zenas had been gone a long time and she missed him.

She got back to the assembly just in time to hear Charlie Goodnight make his toast: an activity he clearly did not enjoy.

"I believe I've found a fine partner," he said, "and I thank him for backing me. Now me and the boys need to go be gathering cattle. Amen."

Bose was waiting with a saddled horse, Nellie Courtright popped out of the crowd and kissed him soundly.

"Did you like that? I thought it might be my last chance," she asked.

"I'm a human being of the male sex—of course I liked it; but the fact is I'm in a hurry and you're married."

"Cowboys waiting in the livery stable," Bose said.

·12·

General Sherman stood looking at the scarred and charred bodies of the teamsters; he looked in silence for a long time. General Mackenzie stood beside them.

The soldiers with them tried not to look at the burnt, slashed bodies, but now and then, they did.

"I was in the Big War, as Mr. Lincoln called it," he said. "I've seen brutality—I've even been dispensed some. But nothin' like this. Tie a man to a wagon tongue and burn his face off, not to mention his other parts."

"They burned the young one's face off, too." He himself felt a little queasy, though he rarely flinched in such situations.

Sherman looked up—to the south was a rocky ridge.

"Unless I am mistaken I came along that ridge to the south yesterday morning."

"We did come along it, sir," Mackenzie said.

"But we caught no whiff of Indians, and we were just an hour or two from Indians. Where were the scouts?" Sherman asked.

"We're so close to Fort Richardson that no one bothered to send them out," Mackenzie said. "They were Kiowa—I guess they don't bother too much about forts."

"I assume they went north—I intend to pursue," Sherman said.

"They went north but slowly," Mackenzie said. "They're proud of their work here. It's my understanding that we've already caught most of them."

"Where?"

"Near the Red River."

"I want them brought to Richardson," Sherman said. "I want them put on trial, and if my schedule permits I want to see them hang."

"I expect we'd all like to see that, sir," Mackenzie said.

"Do you think they could have whipped us, if they'd tried, General Mackenzie?" Sherman asked.

"I have no way of knowing, sir—I didn't see their force," Mackenzie said. In fact he found General Sherman a bit of a pain.

-13-

For once Satank was glad that Satanta was boasting so loudly about the massacre. He bragged so loudly that many of the soldiers listened to him. They had no way of knowing what Satanta said, but they probably knew he was bragging about the tortures he'd inflicted.

Satank sat in a wagon, in the shadows. When no one was looking he chewed at his wrists. The handcuffs were loose—in time he might chew his way free.

Sure enough, just before darkness, he slid the handcuffs off his dirty wrists. The young soldier guarding him was nodding—as soon as he was free Satank grabbed the soldier's knife and stabbed him in the chest. He grabbed a carbine from another soldier and pointed it at him but the carbine didn't fire. Satank threw away the gun and charged the startled soldier with the knife.

"Shoot the old fiend!" a soldier said. Three soldiers fired at once, throwing Satank backward and killing him dead.

"He chewed his own wrists!" one soldier exclaimed.

Several soldiers pointed their rifles at Satanta, who sat very still. He didn't want the soldiers to kill him too, and he knew several wanted to.

The soldiers didn't fire.

Shortly, so as not to scare the soldiers Satanta began to sing a death song.

·14·

Nellie finally found Wyatt at the third saloon she tried. He did not appear to be drunk but had not shaved for several days. There was a glass of whiskey on the table in front of him, but at the moment he was playing solitaire.

"Your family owns a famous saloon—at least the sign is famous. Why are you drinking in this stinky dive when you could be served by your own wife?"

"If she'd serve, it can be touch and go," Wyatt said. Annoying as Nellie could be, there was no denying that she was pretty. Bearing a number of children had not spoiled her figure. If anything she was higher-breasted than Jessie.

"Why the hell should that concern you," he said. "In fact I *like* the smell of this place."

"What's the real reason?" Nellie asked. "If I were guessing I'd say it's Jessie. She's probably trying to restrict your whiskeys in hopes of keeping you healthy."

"My health is better than Doc's—the two of you are welcome to leave me alone," he said.

"I will presently, but Bill Cody would like to have a talk with you—and your brother Morgan was looking for you too."

"Cody? I know you're in love with the old windbag, but why would he want to talk to me?"

"Who I'm in love with is a matter for conjecture," Nellie said. "You're too surly to discuss it with. I'll go get Bill. He's always looking to improve his show, you know," she said. "I think he wants to add a gunfighter skit."

"A what?" Wyatt asked.

"Gunfighter, a gunfighter skit," she said. "Billy the Kid shooting all those people over in New Mexico has made gunfighting real popular with the public and Bill Cody's the best there is at giving the public what it wants. Now that Bill Bonney's dead I guess Bill figures that you and Doc must be the best there is—he always seeks the top talent."

"That's wrong, though, Nellie," Wyatt said. "Top what?" Wyatt asked. "I may have winged a couple of card sharps, up in Dodge, and I've whacked quite a few rowdy cowboys, but I've never done nothing like what happened in New Mexico . . . and neither has Doc."

"Wyatt, it's just acting," Nellie assured him. "You can pull out a pistol and shoot off some blanks, can't you?"

"And the pay might surprise you," she added. "Bill's no cheapskate. And mainly he's just looking for fast draws."

"Fast draws with what, Nellie? Most of my life I don't go armed. You can scare off a lot of cowboys just by looking mean, I guess."

Though Wyatt wanted to tell Nellie Courtright to go jump in the lake, he didn't. In the end he agreed to see Cody, and even promised to bring Doc along, if he could find him. Doc tended to gamble all night and sleep all day, often in a foul hole containing an even fouler woman. Doc was not particular.

For a time Wyatt sat on the porch of the Last Kind Words Saloon and watched the dignitaries file back into the fancy private cars and head back to where dignitaries lived, in Kansas City and elsewhere where they came, summoned to a remote spot by English money.

As the source of the English money, Lord Benny Ernle was still toasting and probably boasting—though Wyatt couldn't hear the toasts or boasts.

The sun began to set—once again, on the prairie, there was the squeal of bagpipes. Lord Ernle did not intend to be without his pipers.

·15·

"You mean stage a holdup?" Doc said. "I'd be wary of it. What if some fool forgot to put blanks in his gun?"

"No, no—no risks," Cody said. "We've done the big fight scenes—Custer's Last Stand for example—hundreds of times with no mistakes. We're experienced show people."

"Maybe you are but I'd want to see all the damn guns," Wyatt said.

"Fine, you can load them yourselves," Cody said.

Wyatt and Doc looked at one another.

"Probably be pretty safe," Wyatt said. "Neither one of us can hit a barn with a pistol, anyway."

"This will mainly involve practice drawing," Cody assured them.

"Now that's plain foolish, Cody," Wyatt said. "If you were headed into gunplay the last thing you'd want is to have your gun stuck in a damn holster, or worse yet in your pocket."

"True," Doc said. "I doubt Billy the Kid had his gun in a damn holster when he went against those killers."

Buffalo Bill Cody smiled—a tired smile though. How to explain to these men, who didn't even seem to be gunmen, that a show had to be real and yet not real at the same time? Of course they were right about frontier gunplay: the fighter would get his gun out and cocked, as he had when he killed the Cheyenne Yellow Hair and claimed the first scalp for Custer.

In the show, of course it was more complicated. The good guys had to win—evil could not be allowed to triumph in a show that had even been enjoyed by Queen Victoria herself, as well as many other crowned heads.

Something similar had just occurred to Wyatt.

"Say me and Doc face off—who gets to win?"

Cody was thinking of Nellie.

"You boys could draw straws or flip coins or something," he said. "Wouldn't work for either one of you to win all the time."

"I could pay each of you one hundred dollars a show."

Doc was taken by surprise.

"One hundred dollars apiece, for shooting blanks at one another?"

Cody nodded.

"Would that be cash?" Wyatt asked.

"Cash," Cody assured him. "You'd have to come to Denver for a while—that's where we're headquartered."

Doc looked at Wyatt.

"What do you think, squire?" he asked.

"I ain't free to think—unlike you. I'd need to clear it with the missus."

"Okay, but be quick about it," Doc said. "We best nail down this job before the real thing comes along."

"And who might the real thing be?" Wyatt asked, with a trace of a smile.

"Just about anybody who likes to shoot and don't mind play-acting," Cody said. "Maybe that fellow from Georgia—Hardin. I think he was a dentist, like yourself."

"Too late, they hung him," Wyatt said.

"He was a lunatic, too," Cody said. "When possible I like to hire people of an unsullied mind. But there are plenty of people out here in the West who are capable of firing off a gun in a show."

"Well, I best be off to see Jessie—I hope I don't wake her up," Wyatt said.

"Henpecked, the great Wyatt Earp," Cody said.

"You evidently don't know Jessie," Wyatt said. "If she's in one of her tempers she'd put a hyena to flight . . ."

"So might I, if I get worked up enough," Nellie said. "That could be the reason my husband lives in the South Seas, if he lives at all."

At the banquet table Lord Ernle was winding up his toasts; the bagpipers once again began to squeal.

"I pride myself on being able to put up with a lot," Nellie said. "But bagpipers are pretty much my limit."

"Want me to shoot one?" Doc asked. "If I'm going to be

working with Cody and trying to hit things with a pistol—or not hit things—I need to be practicing."

"Even if I didn't shoot the bagpipers I could puncture a bag-pipe or two."

"No, no, they're harmless, Doc," Nellie said. "But it is true that they're loud."

·16·

When Wyatt came in, sheepish-looking as usual, Jessie began to steam.

"I've half a mind to throw this whiskey bottle at you," she said.

"I'm glad that it's only half and that the whiskey bottle is better disposed of," Wyatt said. "How about a kiss."

"Are you man enough to try?" she asked.

"I surely think so," Wyatt said, and the next thing they knew they were upstairs, squirming on a bed—in one of the whores' rooms, sort of by accident. At one point she bucked so hard that Wyatt came out, but Jessie caught him with her hand and stuffed him back in—usually she could manage that.

"Oh boy, pleasant," Wyatt said.

"It doesn't make up for everything," Jessie informed him. "You should have taken me to that party. It's the only party there's been around here and you let me sit home."

"Jessie, the dern party was right underneath you," Wyatt said. "All you had to do was step out on the balcony."

"You know what I mean. I might have wanted to show up with my husband."

"So I'm forgetful," Wyatt said. "I'm still your damn husband."

"Even so you don't often perform."

"Maybe my resources are just limited in that line," he said, wondering why women wouldn't just shut up.

"In your case it's mainly that you'd rather drink," she said.

"Let's change the subject, Jessie, we're moving to Denver. Old Bill Cody has offered me and Doc a job in his show."

Jessie sat up and pulled her gown back over her breasts.

"In his show, how?" she asked. "And what would I do?"

"Me and Doc would pretend to be gunfighters and shoot blanks at one another."

"What if they weren't blanks?" Jessie asked.

"Doc thought of that too," Wyatt told her. "Cody swears there'll be no mix-up with the bullets."

"What about me?"

"Denver's a big place—we'll soon find you another bar to tend—might call it the Mile High Saloon, unless Warren shows up with his own sign and wants to invest in a saloon himself."

"Okay," Jessie said. She was sick of Long Grass.

"Is Doc coming?" she wondered.

"I believe he's thinking it over," he said.

"Okay, I'll come," Jessie said.

Denver was bound to be better than where they were.

Then she got up and washed herself.

·17·

Lord Ernle kindly lent Bill Cody a private railroad car to get him back to Kansas, where he could get a train to Denver. At the last minute Nellie jumped in with him, though Denver was in the opposite direction of Rita Blanca, where she lived.

Her reason for traveling a hundred miles in the wrong direction was that it would give her more time with Bill Cody—nobody in her life had meant as much to her as Bill. He had only shown her kindness and had helped her in a million ways.

This evening, as they traveled, she wiped a trickle of tears out of Cody's eyes, using a cotton handkerchief.

"What is it, honey—what is it?" she asked. Cody was looking out the window. Both knew what it was.

"I just tear up when I cross the plains," he said. "Most of my happiest years were spent on the plains. I was here when the plains were so thick with buffalo you could barely ride through them on a horse."

"It must have been a sight," Nellie said.

"Oh yes . . . and the tall grass in Kansas was fine—I won't be seeing it again, I fear. I'm done."

"Don't say that, Bill . . . you know how much I need you," she confessed.

They exchanged a soft kiss . . . it left Nellie fluttery. They were alone in a private car. Her husband, if she still had one, was thousands of miles at sea. They kissed again.

"We've never . . . we've never," she said. "I hate to miss you."

"You didn't miss me, honey," Cody said. "We've done a bunch of kissing, and you've shown me your bosom a few times."

"Oh Bill . . . oh Bill," Nellie said, pulling him close.

Bill Cody put his hand on her and then he went to sleep.

·18·

Goodnight had scarcely swung off his mount when Mary Goodnight burst out of the shack she used for a schoolhouse and gave him an enthusiastic kiss, startling the three towheads Mary had been teaching and probably startling several of the cowboys too. Kissing like that didn't occur every day, in the Palo Duro area.

Odd how women change, he thought. In the several years he spent wooing Mary he had never been allowed such an aggressive kiss. Often, in those days, Mary would turn her head at the last minute, leaving him with only her shoulder to kiss.

"It took you a while to drag yourself back here," Mary told him.

"We hung two horse thieves on the way back—that slowed us down," he said.

He knew at once that the comment was a mistake. Mary jerked back as if she had been quirted.

"How old were they, Charlie?" she asked.

"Old enough to know right from wrong," he said.

"Answer my question!" Mary demanded—she was beginning to color up.

"Twenty-one, at least," he told her. "There were no trees nearby. We caught 'em with the stolen horses and hung them from a telegraph pole," he said. "I don't think it damaged the pole."

"You ruthless bastard, who made you a judge?" she asked.

"But we caught 'em with the stock," he stammered. Mary's rages—and they were not infrequent—always baffled him. He had no idea what to do about them.

"This is a raw place, and you're a raw piece of work yourself, Charlie Goodnight."

"Well, I've not had your education."

"I was talking," she said. "Please have the courtesy not to butt in."

"What do you want?"

"I wish you could bring those boys back to life, but you can't. So I'll give you ten years, if I can stick it out."

"Ten years to do what?"

"To make this into a proper county, with judges and courts and all that goes with a county. And after the courthouse I want a college, where people can learn their algebra. Do those two things in a timely fashion and maybe I won't leave you for brighter climes."

"Not many climes are brighter than this place here," he reminded her. "There is hardly a tree in thirty miles and very damn few clouds that could create cool."

"Don't quibble, Charlie—it don't become you," she said. She turned to leave but stopped again.

"Did you bury those boys proper?" she asked.

Goodnight wondered how he could have blundered so—it was not for the first time, either.

"We were in a hurry," he mumbled.

"Well, those lucky boys—they'll never have to be in a hurry again."

She looked hard at the towheads, and walked away.

Bose had unsaddled Goodnight's horse and
was looking for a stray jar of turpentine. The jar had once
had a proper plug, but the plug had got lost; Bose intended to
replace it with a homemade plug, whittled by himself. While he
looked he heard loud talk behind him, loud talk between Boss
Goodnight and his missus. Bose knew better than to take too
much interest in loud talk between husband and wife.

When the talk stopped and Mary Goodnight went back into
her shack of a schoolhouse Bose saw Boss Goodnight standing
alone. He looked rather defeated, but, of course, such defeats
weren't permanent. And with Boss Goodnight such defeats
were rare.

After a bit he walked over to Bose.

"Well, I lost that fight," Goodnight said. "Did you win many
fights with women, Bose?"

"I don't deal with women, Boss," Bose said. "If there's any around the Palo Duro I don't see them."

"That's what I meant," Goodnight said. "You found a place of safety and I ain't been so provident."

"Still, Miss Mary can cook," Bose reminded him.

Most of Mary's friends called her Molly, not Mary, but Goodnight did not permit himself this intimacy, and Bose followed the practice of his boss; this despite seven years of courtship and eight of marriage.

Mary had her playful moods though—sometimes she even liked to wrestle with him in bed—and she was surprisingly strong. Twice she made his nose bleed. He had never made her nose bleed, though once he did bruise her with his elbow.

"How come you won't call me Molly, like my friends do?" she asked, once.

"Too shy."

"But I'm your wife . . . you pestered me till I gave in. There's no reason you can't call me Molly."

"Too shy," he admitted, and it was God's truth.

"You don't really want me calling you Molly, do you?" he asked, a day or two later.

Mary didn't answer; he didn't call her Molly.

As he was standing with Bose he remembered that Mary had asked him to bring some chalk, and he had remembered it despite Lord Ernle's shindig. He got it out of his saddlebag and took it to the schoolroom: three benches, a blackboard, and a high stool for the teacher.

"Just put it on the bench and don't interrupt," she said, without looking up from her perch. "Right now we're reading about the Rhine maidens.

Goodnight knew that matters were still frosty, all because of two young horse thieves hung from a telegraph pole.

·20·

In the night Mary's sour attitude changed—though less often now that they temporarily lived in the tent, where they had two handsome cots side by side.

"How come when you finally get home all I get is snores?" she wondered; she was a foot from him, in the dark.

"You're sure not much of a hand with women," she added.

Hard as he tried to stay ahead of Mary, mostly he always felt behind. "Here I am, available if I'm handled easy, and what do I get but snores."

"It's the middle of the night—ain't that the usual time for snores?"

"If you slept on your elbow, like I do, you'd be far less likely to snore," she informed him.

"A man lying flat on his back, like you do, is naturally apt to snore."

Goodnight began to get annoyed. Why talk if it was only to gripe at him?

"I should have stayed in Long Grass another month . . . maybe then you'd appreciate me when I showed up."

"Maybe, but even now, late as it is, I might appreciate a visit."

"Do what?"

"A conjugal or connubial visit. If you remember what that is . . . I barely can."

"I don't want to talk all night, Mary."

"I wasn't inviting you to talk," Mary said.

Stumped and somewhat annoyed, Goodnight rolled onto Mary's cot and mounted her—he was surprised by her readiness to be mounted. She was not silent during the mating, either, emitting a screech at the end that must have carried far over the still prairie. Goodnight felt a little embarrassed but Mary at once went to sleep.

At the lots, on his blanket, Bose did hear something coming from the Goodnight tent.

"Miss Molly," he said, smiling to himself.

A young cowboy named Tim heard the sound too—he was sleeping near Bose because he had heard that rattlesnakes wouldn't come near a black man.

"Are they murdering one another?" Tim asked.

"No, and it's none of our business," Bose said.

Two other young cowboys, Willy and John, slept within a circle of lariat ropes because they had heard that a snake would not cross a rope.

Bose knew better. Snakes went where they wanted to go:

they didn't care about white or black and they didn't care about ropes. He himself let snakes be—remove snakes, good and bad, the whole prairie would belong to prairie dogs and pack rats. And resident rattlesnakes rarely struck. Bose often found a snake in his saddle in the morning, and yet he had never been struck.

The moon was full that night—it was the color of a pumpkin—it was almost close enough to touch—that was just how it seemed.

Around five in the morning Bose heard the crunch of boot heels and knew Boss Goodnight was up. He was always up at five—even earlier if he had something important to do.

"I hope those carpenters get here soon—I mean my carpenters, not Lord Ernle's. Mary's not going to tolerate cots much longer, and I don't blame her. I've got a crick in my back from sleeping on a damn cot as it is."

"Lady like Miss Mary needs a house of her own," Bose said.

"She ain't a Miss," Goodnight said. "And you can call her Molly—I can't seem to."

"Sometimes a lady don't want to be a lady," he said, mainly to himself.

"Do you care, boss?" Bose asked.

"No," Goodnight admitted. "The damn expense of a full-time lady would soon leave me busted."

Bose picked up the rope and went to catch the horses, though it was barely light enough for him to throw a loop.

·21·

Goodnight was stepping off a patch of prairie where he meant to build his principal cattle pens when he saw a familiar figure riding in from the south.

"Here comes Chief Quanah," Bose said. "Looks like he's found another buffalo calf for your missus."

"I'm trying to count," Goodnight insisted. "The less I'm interrupted the fewer mistakes I'll make."

"Besides," he added, "I see Quanah everywhere. I can't line up at a bank without he's there ahead of me, putting in money."

But he was polite when Quanah arrived with the calf.

"You might take that calf on to Mrs. Goodnight," he said. "She's in the buffalo business, thanks to you. I'm busy with the cattle business."

"That was after you washed out as Indian fighters," Quanah said. "All of you except Mackenzie."

Goodnight was remembering that his wife had said more than once that she thought Quanah was probably the best-looking man in America. It didn't mean Quanah *was* the best-looking man in America; it just meant that Mary Goodnight was prone to rash statements.

"Tell me again what happened on the Pease River," Quanah asked. "Because of that I had to do without a mother for the rest of my life."

"I suppose you can't help dwelling on it," Goodnight said. "I was a Ranger then—we hit a camp that was mostly women and children. The Comanche women were running for their lives. A cowboy was about to shoot your mother when I looked close and saw that she was blue-eyed—I yelled and nobody shot."

"I wish you'd left her—she was happy with the People."

"She was the most famous white captive in Texas—we couldn't leave her," Goodnight said. "Her family—your family too, I guess—had been looking for her for twenty years almost."

Bose came walking over.

"Morning, chief," Bose said. He reached to take the buffalo calf, but Quanah drew back.

"I want to give it to Miss Molly myself," he said.

"And she ain't Miss anything, she's my wife," Goodnight said.

"Everybody but you call her Molly," Quanah said. "What have you got against the name?"

Goodnight didn't answer. He went and saddled his horse.

"He's hard to get along with in the morning," Quanah observed.

"Little grouchy sometimes," Bose admitted.

To the north, two miles, was the emerging shell of Lord Ernle's castle. Quanah had heard about it in Washington, from Lord Ernle himself, at a big reception to announce the big international partnership. Still, he hadn't expected it to be so big. He was skeptical of the notion of a big cattle empire, himself. Cattle were too slow to grow and couldn't handle the severe plains winters, as had been demonstrated a few winters back when fifty million dollars' worth of cattle froze to death on the northern plains. If anybody could make cattle work, it would probably be Goodnight, but Quanah remained skeptical.

Quanah himself was more interested in the social possibilities, as represented by the vast castle going up. He had never been in a castle before and looked forward to visiting Lord Ernle.

"I hear Lord Ernle has a fine-looking woman with him . . . know anything about her?"

"She's tall," Bose said. "That about all I know about her."

"I like tall women," Quanah said. "Most of my wives are stocky. I hear Lord Ernle is bringing greyhounds . . . I'm hoping to take Lord Ernle on a wolf hunt. Do you know when he's expected?"

"Don't know," Bose said. He himself had not been in the fight on the Pease River when Quanah's mother, Cynthia Ann Parker, had been retaken by the Rangers, but he had seen her several times around Austin and he had never seen a sadder woman. Her eyes held no life, no hope. When, one day, he heard she had died, he felt sure it must have been a relief.

"If San Saba is as tall as they say she is I might ask her to be my wife. I've only got three," Quanah said.

"Three more than I've got," Bose thought.

· 22 ·

Flo had always wondered about something but had never got up her nerve to ask about it, and that was that San Saba always wore a sock on her right foot—a thick sock that she pulled halfway up her calf. She even wore it in the bath, and she bathed every day—at least she did when the water supply permitted.

San Saba never took off her sock. Otherwise she was careless about her body.

The day they were supposed to leave for the great new ranch in Texas, San Saba noticed Flo looking at her sock. She was just stepping out of her bath. The sock, of course, was wet. The girl Flo was special to her, so without hesitation San Saba stooped and peeled off the sock.

There were red markings low on San Saba's right ankle. Flo was disturbed, without knowing exactly what she was seeing.

"It's a brand," San Saba explained. "I very rarely show it."

"Who branded you?"

"The eunuchs, when I was six."

"I guess it hurt."

San Saba smiled.

"It still hurts," she said. "But now you know my darkest secret. Could you bring me another sock?"

Lord Ernle, meanwhile, was directing the departure of his large, complicated entourage, which filled a number of wagons, buggies, and other conveyances. There were his pipers, of course, and a fowler and a falconer, and a man to handle the greyhounds. There were two blacksmiths, two cooks, three Irish laundresses, and even an electrician: it was clear to Lord Ernle that electricity was the coming thing and he wanted to see to it that his Texas establishment was absolutely state-of-the-art.

"No half measures," he muttered several times. It was his personal motto; he intended to have it latinized and put on a crest.

San Saba watched it all from her balcony: beyond the tiny town there was the vastness of the plains: colorless, gloomy, vast: the sea of grass, Lord Ernle called it.

Benny Ernle kept looking at her hopefully, at the dinner table. For years she had summoned her gaiety to enliven Benny Ernle's meals. The food was excellent: pheasant again, and rabbit, fresh killed. She chose the rabbit, and ate in silence.

"What? Not off your feed?" Lord Ernle asked.

"We've a hard journey ahead of us—I would be foolish to overeat," she said.

Her mood alarmed him—it was a change he hadn't ordered.

"Bosh, I overeat every night," he told her. "Where's your smile? Your laughter?"

San Saba looked at him directly; perhaps as directly as her mother had looked at the sultan, when she refused him.

Lord Ernle made an excuse and left the table.

It would not be the end of it, San Saba knew. Lord Ernle must not be thwarted, ever. San Saba felt sure there would be punishment, just as there had been for her mother, the Rose Concubine.

DENVER

·23·

The gunfighter skit involving Wyatt and Doc did not, at first, go well at all. For one thing the pair had not bothered to practice—both despised practice, on the whole.

"Pull a pistol out of a dern holster and shoot it—why would that require practice?" Wyatt wondered.

"Everything about show business requires practice," Cody told him, but he didn't press the point; these moody men would find out soon enough about the practicalities of show business.

Sure enough, on the very first draw, Wyatt yanked his gun out so vigorously that it somehow flew out of his hand and landed twenty feet in front of him with the barrel in the dirt.

Doc, meanwhile, had the opposite problem: he had jammed his pistol in its holster so tight that it wouldn't come out. This behavior annoyed Doc so much that he ripped off the holster and threw it at a bronc, which happened to be loose in the arena.

The crowd was largely silent: this was not what they had expected; many members of the audience were eager to get on to the dramatic reenactment of Custer's Last Stand.

Some bronc riders and a cowboy or two snickered, which did not improve Wyatt's mood, or Doc's—or Bill Cody's.

"They've made it into a comedy routine," he said to Frank, Annie Oakley's husband, who happened to be nearby.

"It was not meant to be a comedy routine."

The second night went little better. Some prop man filled Doc's gun with blanks but forgot to do the same with Wyatt's. Doc then shot Wyatt six times while Wyatt snapped his useless pistol six times.

The third night they finally got it right, firing a crescendo of blanks; but the crowd showed little interest. Some called for Wyatt to toss his pistol again.

By the fifth night they were getting fairly good at the fast draw, but on the sixth night Cody came in with a desperate look on his face; he told them that Harry Tammen, the magnate who owned the show and most of Colorado, had concluded that public interest was waning, and the show closed down.

"Closed it down—you mean we're out of work?" Wyatt asked.

"You're out of work and I'm out of everything except the clothes on my back," Cody said.

"He's running a sheriff's sale tomorrow. I think he even plans to sell my horse."

"Why the son of a bitch," Doc said. "What if I go shoot him?"

Cody merely looked doleful.

Wyatt and Doc had developed a fondness for the old show-man.

"Why Bill, that's rotten," Wyatt said. "What will you do?"

"Go home and quarrel with Lulu," Cody said. "That's my wife, who lives in Buffalo, in the state of New York."

"As for you gunfighters, there are other shows." Cody said. "Texas Jack might hire you, and there's plenty of gambling dens here in Denver."

"No, I guess we'll amble down the road," Wyatt said. "Jessie's getting nosebleeds from the altitude."

Cody gave a little wave and turned away.

"We ought to kill that fellow Tammen," Wyatt said. "He's about to put Bill Cody in his grave."

"I don't favor gambling much more here," Doc said. "Competition's too advanced. I've been playing steady for two weeks and I'm just up eighty dollars, and you know how dangerous I am at the poker table."

"I admit you're fair," Wyatt said. "Farther than fair I don't go."

"Where will we strike next, boys?"

He was addressing three of his brothers: Morgan, Virgil, and Warren—the latter had brought his Last Kind Words sign with him; all he needed was a saloon to hang it on.

"Virg has been offered the sheriffing job in Tombstone," Morgan said. "And he could hire me to deputy."

"So I guess me and Warren can just be left out," Wyatt said.

"But you don't like sheriff work—or any work," Virgil said.

"True, but I have an even greater dislike of starving," Wyatt said.

"There's Mobetie, it's a damn sight closer than Tombstone," Morgan said. "I'm told there's no law there yet, and no order either. Wyatt wouldn't be subjecting his lovely wife to high altitudes."

"Mobetie, I have no idea of such a place," Doc admitted.

"Oh, it's Goodnight's country—it's probably somewhere on his ranch. I'm sure it's windy," Morgan said.

"Ain't you a dandy," Wyatt said. "I suspect you know pretty much all there is to know."

"Far from it," Morgan declared.

What he did know was when his brother Wyatt was itching to start a fight—any fight. It was partly the way he hunched his shoulders when he sat, and partly the chill look in his eyes.

On such occasions—and they were frequent—the prudent thing to do was leave, and Morgan did.

·24·

The only person who hated the high-altitude nosebleeds in Denver more than Jessie was Wyatt, who turned plenty pale at the mere sight of blood. Once while they were at it her nose began to spout blood which got on Wyatt's chest and on his clothes.

"Oh goddamnit!" he said, and before they were even finished Wyatt pulled out and ran off. She didn't see him for a week. Wyatt threatened to leave her so often she thought he might have finally done it, but he hadn't. He had just been salooning, maybe whoring, though maybe not whoring. Wyatt was not easily pleasured—Jessie knew she was finally going to have to look elsewhere for her romance, and the first place she intended to look was Virgil, who could rarely get close to Jessie without his tongue hanging out.

Still, Jesse knew she had to be careful. The Earps might

quarrel among themselves, but they were quick to unite when there was a threat—even just a social threat.

Wyatt looked awful when he showed back up—he always did after a binge. Cleanliness meant little to Wyatt, though it meant much to Morgan, who always wore creased trousers and a starched shirt.

Once or twice Jessie had tried to steal a kiss from Virgil, but the results had been disappointing. Doc Holliday had never given her the time of day either. If she really put her mind to it she could usually provoke a little scuffle with Wyatt—and better to fight with her husband than just spend her days pouring whiskey from a bottle to a glass.

"The future's settled for a while," Wyatt told her.

"What future?"

"You and me and Warren are going to visit a town called Mobetie, which is probably in Texas."

"What about Doc?"

"Doc's slow to make a decision," he said. "I expect he'll join us eventually."

"Why Mobetie?"

"Why not? It's a brand-new town. Warren is carrying around his sign, hoping to find a saloon to hang it on," Wyatt said.

"Will I have a job . . . bartender, barmaid?"

"We'll see about it," he said.

That afternoon Jessie let a photographer take her picture. The photographer had a studio. It was boredom that drove her to it. He made her dress like an Indian, which she wasn't. But it passed the afternoon. In one shot you could see her breasts and even her nipples. Probably Wyatt wouldn't like that very much. But, by good luck, he never saw that picture—at least not until years later, when it showed up in an Arizona magazine. The reason Jessie got away with it at the time was because Wyatt and Warren were anxious to get off to this place called Mobetie, which was in Texas.

The first night out it snowed. All they had to make a fire with were cow chips, which didn't make a very warm fire. Jessie didn't care. At least they were going downhill and her nose had finally stopped bleeding.

Charles and Mary Goodnight were showing Lord Ernle, their English partner, around the ranch they owned together. They were riding across the breaks of the Canadian River, thick at this season with wild plum bushes. The plums were not quite ready to pick.

"I wouldn't mind having a wild plum bush around our house, if we ever get a house," Mary said. "Do you think they could be transplanted, Charlie?"

"If you had somebody willing to dig up a plum bush I expect they could be transplanted," he said.

Just then Lord Ernle's greyhounds put up two lobo wolves—in a moment both the greyhounds and the wolves were in full cry.

Goodnight studied the chase, which was taking place in very broken country. They were on the edge of the Palo Duro Canyon, with ravines and drop-offs aplenty. Lord Ernle was riding his thoroughbred, an unstable animal at best, in Goodnight's view.

"Thoroughbreds might be all right for Scotland or someplace level—but not here," he said.

"I don't think Scotland's particularly level," Mary said.

It's just like her to argue, he thought, but he held his tongue.

"Most places are more level than the caprock," he said, civilly he thought.

Vaguely troubled, he began to lope in the direction of the chase. Benny Ernle was a skilled rider, of course, but he didn't know the country. He had begun to spur up a little when suddenly the greyhounds disappeared. Lord Ernle was brandishing a pig sticker when he too disappeared.

Goodnight spurred up, but he knew what he would find before he found it. The drop-off, when he came to it, was sheer and about twenty feet. At the bottom the thoroughbred was trying to rise, on broken forelegs; two of the greyhounds had suffered the same fate. Lord Ernle lay flat on his back, dead. There was no sign of the wolves.

Mary, a careful rider, showed up a little later.

"Oh, Charlie, my god," she said.

An old, short, very dirty man was bending over Lord Ernle; he carried a short knife and had been skinning a skunk.

"Why it's Caddo Jake!" she exclaimed. "It's his shack I use for my school."

"Skunks are plentiful along the Canadian," Goodnight reminded her. "That's about all Jake traps."

A hundred yards west they found a little trail down the cap-rock; they went down it carefully and hurried to the bodies.

"Who was that fool?" Jake asked. "He came flying off that bluff and nearly hit me."

"An Englishman," Goodnight said. "Has he moved?"

"No, and he ain't going to—neck's broke," Jake said.

"Now I don't have a rich partner," Goodnight thought.

Mary had begun to cry.

·26·

The minute San Saba saw Benny Ernle's body, which was brought back in a wagon, she knew that her life was in mortal peril—and Flo's life too. The butler, the farrier, the cook, the blacksmith—all the men who worked for Benny were looking at her silently. She had been Benny's favorite for a long time. She had ordered them all around, been queenly, sharp, harsh as the occasion demanded it. Now if they could catch her she would pay, and not just with the normal lusts. Old Hamid, who took care of the dairy goats, was said to have been a torturer in his youth. San Saba didn't want him practicing his ancient skills on her body or Flo's.

The Goodnights were her only hope and she at once approached them.

"Mrs. Goodnight, I'd like to come work for you and I'd like to bring Flo. I assure you we'll be a useful pair, and if we stay here we're lost."

Mary looked at the men ringing the courtyard: she saw what San Saba meant. The men were looking at the two women, the one not exactly black, the other not exactly white.

Charles Goodnight didn't see the looks. What he didn't see was why, having lost one partner, he should acquire two women.

"Hire them to do what?" he said stiffly. "We don't even have a house yet."

"Yes you do, there's this one," Mary said. "It's on your land—you could just claim it."

"Claim this pile, why we'd rattle around in it like gourds," Goodnight said; but, in a minute, he saw that the idea had some merit.

"We could start our college in it, and maybe a courthouse too. I guess we'd have to round up a town of sorts before it would work."

"Come to think of it, there's Mobetie," Goodnight said. "It's small enough to be readily moved."

"We can sew and cook and launder, and I could even help you teach school. I have fluent Spanish, which you Texans will be needing pretty soon."

Mary Goodnight clapped.

"See, Charlie?" she asked. "Just yesterday I heard you telling Benny that you'd soon need somebody to speak Mexican so you can keep track of the vaqueros on the long drives out of south Texas; and now here's someone showed up."

"Besides all that I'm pretty good at breaking horses," San Saba said.

"A woman break horses?" Goodnight said, startled yet again.

"Yes, an old gaucho taught me," she said. "Benny owned a million acres of the pampas, and more cattle than you've got in Texas."

"What? I doubt it," Goodnight protested.

"It's true though," she said. "I came to love the pampas—they're not unlike this country here. And the beef was excellent."

"I've heard that, but I've not yet had time to visit," he said.

"I am no hand at breaking horses," he added. "Most of my remuda is half broke and dangerous to the cowhands."

"Try me then, Mr. Goodnight—I can do what I claim."

Mary hugged San Saba, who hugged her in turn.

"Let's hire them, Charlie—I'm tired of being the only respectable woman in this part of the country."

It was on the tip of Goodnight's tongue to question the respectability of two of the three, but he realized that Mary did need company and it wouldn't do to be too picky. Besides, in his years on the plains he had often seen whores go on to become excellent wives to some farmer or cowhand; better wives in some cases than women with unblemished records in all departments.

"I'll hire them if you say so, Mary," he said. "I guess eventually we'll figure out what they've been hired to do. I hope they don't mind rough camping, though—that's what it's gonna be, for a while."

"We don't mind," San Saba said.

Mary hugged the Creole girl, too.

"You two can call me Molly," she said. "That's what Chief Quanah calls me—and my friends as well."

"What does the Colonel call you?" San Saba asked on a whim.

Mary burst out laughing.

"What would he be a colonel of?" she said. "When he's not cussin' he calls me Mary, but I'm Molly to my friends."

"Fine name," San Saba said.

MOBETIE

·27·

As Wyatt and Doc were approaching Mobetie, on a day that was very dusty they ran into a small hunched man making a modest camp near the Canadian River. He was skinning a skunk at the time and had forty or fifty more hides piled up behind him. He showed no apprehension when they showed up; in fact he even offered them a stew he had prepared. The stew was in an Indian bowl—which tribe neither of them knew.

"I'm Caddo Jake, I live by the skunk," the old trapper said. "Care to buy my hides?"

"No, and for that matter anything can wind up in a stew," Doc said.

"It's jackrabbit in this one," Caddo Jake said.

"Oh, well that's different," Doc said, helping himself to a bowl of the stew, which he enjoyed.

"Caddo Jake's a known fibber, I expect you just ate skunk," Wyatt said.

They had stopped to count the buildings in Mobetie—it didn't take long.

"I just count seven," Wyatt went on. "And one of them's a barbershop."

"All you have to do to acquire a barbershop is shoot the barber, which I'll be glad to do," Doc said.

"It's my experience that people will shoot dentists even quicker than barbers," Wyatt said. "Let's find a saloon and soak our tonsils."

They were about to go in one of the battered little frame buildings when a cowboy on a bay horse came surging through the swinging doors. The bay jumped the little porch and went tearing down the street; then it broke into bucking and quickly managed to throw the cowboy.

"That cowboy's name is Teddy Blue, he works for Shanghai Pierce, or did," Wyatt said.

"I don't know him, neither," Doc said. "That cowboy nearly trampled me—we ought to at least go pummel him."

"If there's ever a restless cowboy it's Teddy," Wyatt said. "I tried to arrest him once in Dodge, but he got on with a herd and went all the way to Montana. I didn't know he was back on the plains until I saw him ride out that door."

"Montana's a fine place to freeze to death, I hear," Doc said.

"I need to travel with someone better educated," Wyatt said. "There are few subjects you can even discuss intelligently."

"I don't claim to know much: cards, fucking, and dentistry about covers it," Doc said.

"I entrusted my wife to my brother Warren, I hope he gets

her here safe," Wyatt said. "What's the best thing we can do while we're waiting for them to get here?"

"If you're not going to let me pull teeth, then next best recreation would be to get drunk."

"I vote for drunk," Doc said.

·28·

Teddy Blue, having been decisively thrown, lay for a while in the main street of Mobetie, Texas. Fortunately none of his fellow cowboys noticed his weak performance as a bronc rider. He had ridden his horse into the saloon on a dare from a whore—his practice was always to accept dares; it spiced life up a little. As he lay in the street, very drunk, he could hear laughter, though nothing seemed particularly funny to him. He had drunk plenty of whiskey; when he awoke it was to find none other than Wyatt Earp dragging him to safety at the side of the street.

"You'd be better off living in Montana, Blue," Wyatt said. "You're too young to be run over in a damn worthless place like Mobetie."

"I need a job," Teddy said. "Know of any herds heading north?"

"Blue, I just got here, and besides I ain't a cattleman," Wyatt said. "I don't keep up with herds."

"Charlie Goodnight's probably got some, but he's stiff, I hear. Don't he own the panhandle now?"

Teddy's head began to throb—the whiskey he drank had been of a low quality.

"Are you conscious?" Wyatt asked.

Teddy saw the whore who had made the dare; she was on the porch of the saloon, looking at him. Her name was Emma. She was small but vigorous. And she was sweet on him.

It took Doc and Wyatt both to get Teddy Blue solidly back on his feet, but when he was upright he went back across the street to see Emma. As soon as he sobered enough he meant to collect on his dare.

·29·

A week after Lord Ernle's death in Palo Duro Canyon, Buffalo Bill Cody died in Denver. Nellie Courtright tapped out the news on a special telegraph key provided to her at Cody's request. Nellie had been nervous. She wept so hard at the news that she could barely see the special key, and, in any case, she had not been a practicing telegrapher in years; but Cody insisted and she could not deny him. All in all he had been fine with her, really fine. Often they joked about marrying, without doing anything about it.

Nellie was by then writing for a number of magazines, some of them steady customers. Not an hour after she tapped out "Buffalo Bill is dead" to a grieving world she got a telegram from the *New York Sun*, asking her to go to Texas and write about the great castle on the Canadian River that a cattleman named Charles Goodnight now seemed to own. Of course Nellie remembered the Goodnights—once she had impulsively kissed Charlie, she remembered. She was needing money just then—she had six girls to educate and clothe so she immediately took the job.

The railroad would take her most of the way; for the rest she hired a buggy.

Goodnight had busied himself by providing ample pens for the thousands of cattle he planned to bring up the trail. Nellie was not surprised to see the huge pen, but she was surprised to see San Saba in a smaller pen with several wiry-looking mustangs. She wore a large hat and a leather skirt and was trying to get one of the mustangs to accept the halter—the horse eventually did, and she led it over to the fence.

Goodnight and Mary met her on the steps of the vast shell of a house—there were tents in the great hall.

"Hurrah, it's Nellie, my favorite visitor," Mary said.

"Probably your only visitor," Nellie said. She did not bug Charlie and wondered if he remembered her impulsive kiss. It was hard to know much about Charlie, though he did seem to consider himself the boss of the panhandle.

"I'm off to south Texas to round up a herd," he said. "What did you want here, Miss Courtright?"

"Charlie, we've known one another a good long while," she said. "Can't you even call me by my first name?"

"Yes, do it, you big fool," Mary told him.

"I was brought up a certain way and it wasn't the way you two was brought up," he said.

Just then Bose walked up with Goodnight's horse.

"Hi, Bose," Nellie said. "Charlie I have to write about you for *Collier's* magazine," she said. "What do you have to say about the late Lord Ernle?"

"He should have watched where he was going," Goodnight said. He mounted and rode away.

"A girl could wait a long time for a goodbye kiss," Mary said. She sounded annoyed.

"I saw San Saba in a pen with some mustangs," Nellie said. "That's unusual."

"It is," Mary allowed. "None of Charlie's horse breakers like to deal with mustangs so he let San Saba have a try and she seems to be doing a fine job, which surprised Charlie no end."

At dusk they ate a simple meal of greens, mainly, using only a tiny corner of the great table Lord Ernle had brought in. They also had the rump of a young antelope.

"It's rather like veal," San Saba said. Flo ate with them—Mary liked her and had persuaded her to cut her hair. In one little room of the great house they found an immense quantity of powders, unguents, lotions, and the like. Nellie, who paid attention to her appearance, was amazed by the profusion.

"All this and only three females to use them," she said.

"Oh, Benny brought that stuff for his boys," San Saba said. "He liked to have five or six around—and call me Saba, I'll call you Nellie."

Nellie knew there were men who favored boys, but she didn't know where Lord Ernle would have found any in the empty panhandle of Texas.

"I've got this magazine to satisfy, Saba," Nellie said. "Wouldn't you at least let me do an article about you? I'll be discreet, I promise."

San Saba smiled and changed the subject.

·30·

Sultry nights and lightning were bad things on a cattle drive, Goodnight knew. He insisted that his cowhands keep their horses on a short rope at such times, as a precaution against stampedes. It was the right thing to do, but not all cowboys were wise enough to do it, some were unable to sleep with a horse practically right over them.

Goodnight was renowned in Texas for his vision, which few could equal. Once his own wife Mary held up a cattle drive for several hours because she and the trail boss thought they saw Indians. Goodnight arrived, glanced at the Indians, cussed for a while before informing Mary and the trail boss that what they saw was merely a pair of yucca plants.

Goodnight's hearing was the equal of his eyesight, and on this particular night it was his hearing that saved him. To the west he heard a thunderclap and the sky went white with lightning; before it fully darkened the cattle were up and running. Goodnight yelled a warning, then he swung on his horse and ran; the thunder in the heavens was soon drowned out by the hoofbeats of thousands of cattle.

The stampede filled the plains; cattle were running on a front fifty miles across. What Goodnight knew that the cowboys didn't was that three huge herds were stampeding: his, a herd belonging to cattleman Shanghai Pierce, and one belonging to Dan Wagoner. There could be as many as ten thousand cattle running—maybe more.

Some stampedes could be turned, if the cowboys were skilled enough. But there was no turning this mass, Goodnight knew. In a lightning flash he saw Bose, fifty yards away and running for his life. Blue balls of static lightning ran along the horns of some of the cattle.

Goodnight's deep-chested gelding Mackenzie—he was named for the great cavalry officer Ranald Mackenzie—had as much wind as any horse. Goodnight was no trained bareback rider; he could only cling to the gelding's mane. If he fell off he'd be dead. Fortunately the plain was level, with few dips.

At the castle the women sat on the unfinished porch, chatting late. Nellie made a few notes—she intended to write about the now-abandoned castle.

"You don't know what a luxury this is for me," Mary said. "Having women to talk to. Talking to Charlie is much like talking to a stump."

San Saba was weaving; abruptly she stopped.

"What is it?" Mary said. She suddenly had the sense that the earth itself was moving. The porch they sat on began to shake a little.

"It's cattle," San Saba said. "We best get in that tower Benny had built. Quick."

"Good lord," Nellie said. She could just see a kind of mass, to the south.

"Quick, quick, quick," San Saba said, pulling Flo with her. She began to herd the women up the stairs into the strange tower Benny had had built. She was just in time too: cattle began to surge through the castle, smashing the great table. A steer tried to come up the stairs behind, but his long horns wouldn't allow him into the stairwell.

"It's a flood of cattle," Nellie said—the whole castle shook from their passage.

Just as Nellie thought the whole structure might collapse the tide of animals began to ebb. The lightning still flashed, but not so close by: the distant plains danced with lightning.

In one of the flashes Mary saw Bose, carefully making his way through the remnants of the herd, toward the castle.

"Trust Bose to come through," Mary said. "Charlie says he's the best cowboy there is."

"Even better than himself?" Nellie asked.

"I don't think Charlie considers himself a cowboy—Charlie mainly considers himself a boss."

It occurred to Mary that Charlie just might be dead. He had told her many times that anybody can be dead, and dead any day.

It could just be a matter of a man's luck running out.

In the lightning flashes she could see the carcasses of a dozen or more cattle, trampled to death by the surviving herd.

Mary got a lantern going and the light caused Bose to lope over their way.

"Glad you made it, Bose, where's Charlie?" Mary asked.

"Don't know," Bose said. "He was riding bareback, off east of me. Then I didn't see him again."

Mary felt a stab of fear. Her husband might well be dead. For all her griping at him, she really did love him.

"He might have gone back and tried to find his saddle," Bose said.

"Anybody killed?"

Her imagination was in full flower—she was imagining her husband dead.

Nellie Courtright had the same thought. Lord Ernle, Bill Cody, and now Charlie.

"Could you go find him, Bose? I'm plenty worried," Mary said.

"I'll find him," Bose said. "Probably just looking for that saddle."

"And hurry please," Mary said.

Bose nodded, but he didn't like to hurry; once he was out of sight of the ladies he slowed down, and took his time.

·31·

"We're lucky this town had a good-sized tree," Doc said. He was speaking about Mobetie, Texas, the town with one tree. He and Wyatt had just been concluding a successful night of card playing when the stampede arrived. The cowboys knew what it was—Teddy Blue was out the door and on horseback in seconds; but some of the gamblers were not so quick: they milled around in the street and three of them paid the ultimate price for it: they were trampled to jelly. Fortunately Wyatt remembered the one tree and the two of them got up in it just as the surge of cattle filled the street.

"Too many goddamn cattle," Doc said, but no one heard him.

Wyatt had supposed he was alone in the tree, except for Doc; but then he felt something bump him. It felt like a head; in the next flash he saw that it *was* a head; indeed, two heads: twisted heads with bodies attached.

"Oh my god, we climbed the hanging tree," he said, after which he immediately jumped to the ground, twisting an ankle in the process. It was several minutes before he could stand up but by then the big stampede had subsided.

"They're just carcasses," Doc pointed out. He himself had descended rather hastily but did himself no damage that he could find.

Dawn was breaking—the clarity of early morning lit the vast plain. Wyatt looked up at the two cadavers: both of them were young.

"I wonder if Teddy Blue made it to safety—or Charlie Goodnight," he said.

As the light improved it was possible to see that, though the cattle had stopped running, hundreds of them were still there.

"There's hundreds of cattle around Mobetie," Wyatt said. "We could cut off a hundred or so and start a ranch. Jessie could be the cook."

"No," Doc said. "I abhor the mere presence of cattle."

"It would be easy money," Wyatt reminded him.

"Once you get beyond a milk cow you've got too many cattle," Doc said.

"You wouldn't have to milk any," Wyatt said. "Maybe we could get Teddy Blue to come cowboy for us."

"The day he starts is the day I part company with you boys," Doc said.

"Oh, forget it," Wyatt said. "We'll just go on to Arizona."

·32·

Jessie soon regretted that she had chosen to travel with Warren Earp, who was no talker. The longer the two of them jogged along in their buggy, the less Warren said. They learned about the big stampede from a cowboy who didn't bother to give his name. He did mention to them that three huge herds had got mixed together, somewhere near Mobetie.

"You'll be seeing dead cattle here and there," he said. "Got trampled under."

The cowboy was right. They began to see carcasses here and there, being pecked at by crows. Many crows, many flies.

Warren skirted the carcasses, but made no comment. He had his sign, the one that said The Last Kind Words Saloon. It filled the back end of the buggy, but Jessie, who had few clothes, didn't mind.

Tired of silence, Jessie thought she might tease Warren a

little—after all he was probably her brother-in-law, depending on whether Wyatt had actually been divorced when he and Jessie married.

"If we come on a saloon, what do we do: go in and make sure no kind words are spoken, and if not you'll hang up your sign."

"Silent Warren" the whores called him, and often. Warren was noted for his inability to resist the girls.

The deeper into them Jessie got, the more the plains depressed her. It would have been better to take the train to California and come to Arizona from the west, as Virgil and Morgan had done. Morgan always had a job, usually marshaling, though once he ran a fire department in Kansas City.

"Tombstone, Arizona," Warren said, as if it meant something.

"That's not what Wyatt said," Jessie insisted. "Wyatt said we were settling in Texas."

Before Warren answered they saw some antelope, about twenty.

"Better than venison," Warren said, picking up his rifle. But the antelope were skittish and they could never get close enough for a shot.

Goodnight grimly backtracked through dead and dying cattle until he found his saddle, which had been trampled badly, as he had expected. It was no big loss—he could get another saddle easily enough. What he could not afford to lose, however, was his brand book, which was in his saddlebag, unharmed. The book contained the specifics of more than two hundred brands: his several and several more belonging to Dan Wagoner and Shanghai Pierce. Goodnight knew that the run had involved at least eight thousand cattle: without the brand books it would be virtually impossible to sort them out. And it would very likely take a full week in any case. It was time lost but there was no help for it.

But there was a lesson to be learned from the mix-up. Neither he nor Pierce nor Wagoner were particularly cooperative men, but they *were* greedy stockmen. What had just been demonstrated was that it was unwise to have three herds in close proximity. The plains allowed for a great deal of spreading out. And at least he had a good brand book, which is more than Dan Wagoner could say—when Goodnight came up on him he and three cowboys were digging a grave.

"How many did you lose, Charlie?" Wagoner asked. He was a short man, but durable.

"I don't know yet," Goodnight said. "But I have my brand book—I expect it will be helpful."

"What about Pierce?" he asked.

"Ain't seen him, but he's probably off somewhere drinking whiskey," Wagoner said.

Then he turned briefly to the freshly dug grave—with a nod he summoned his cowboys and invited them to take off their hats.

Goodnight took off his hat.

"This was Johnny Deakin, a good boy of sixteen I believe," Wagoner said. "He rode through a prairie dog town, an infernal thing for a cowboy to encounter at night. His horse broke a leg and the cattle stampeded right over young Johnny. Such is the life and death of a good cowboy. Amen."

Goodnight remembered the boy, who had twice asked for a job, and was turned down on grounds that he was too young. He had refused him; now he felt some regret. Many a fine cowhorse had broken a leg in a prairie dog town. Life was a peril, purely a peril.

"We'll have to sort this out, Dan," Goodnight said. "I've got pens enough for one herd but not for three. We're looking at a week of sorting, at least."

Later in the day he found Shanghai Pierce, who was being guided by Caddo Jake.

"Lost my skunk hides, had fifty-two," Caddo Jake said.

"You may have lost the hides but you ain't lost the smell," Shanghai Pierce said. "The smell of every goddamn one lingers with you."

Goodnight informed Pierce, whom he had never liked particularly, that he had his brand book and so the sorting could start the next day. His cowboys would be on hand to assist the work.

"I lost three cowboys," Pierce informed him. "Wagoner lost one—you're lucky that your full crew survived."

"It's too early to say," Goodnight said. He was not certain about his own cowboy count until Bose Ikard showed up later in the day and said all hands had survived.

"We're lucky," he told Bose, at which point he realized that in his concern for his hands he had totally forgotten his wife and the women who were with her.

"Oh damn," he said. "I got to thinking about the cowboys and totally forgot Mary and the girls."

Bose was silent. He had not known what to tell the women. Anyway, once they saw him, what they wanted to know was about Boss Goodnight. "Maybe you could go tell 'em I'll be home when I get these cattle sorted," Goodnight said.

Bose didn't answer. Goodnight knew that meant he didn't think much of his idea.

"Oh hang it!" Goodnight said. "Mary will never let me live this down. I might as well go take some of my medicine now."

And off he went, in a lope.

·34·

Jessie was uncomfortable in the presence of respectable women—she didn't know why. It's true that she herself
had been born in a whorehouse in Kentucky—at least that was
what her grandmother told her; but she had never sold herself
for money, though in the barkeeping environment where she
worked she often got offers that were in no way proper.

Wyatt told her once that if he ever caught her whoring he
would shoot her in the back of the head.

"That way you'd never see it coming—that's the best I can
give you," he said.

"Sneak," she said, and he was one too. Sleepy and careless as
he seemed, Wyatt didn't miss much.

She and Warren buggied up to the great prairie castle just at
suppertime and were promptly asked to take a meal.

San Saba was quiet, but Nellie Courtright chattered away.

"I'll be glad when Charlie shows up," she said. "I'd like to know how many cattle ran in that stampede—I think it was probably the worst stampede ever. I'd write an article about it if I had more information."

Mary Goodnight gave a kind of snort.

"Charlie Goodnight don't release information," she said. "If I asked him which boot he put on first he'd put me off."

Jessie found it puzzling: why would anyone care which boot a man put on first? But Nellie was a pretty woman, and pretty women had a strong effect on any of the Earps, particularly Warren.

"I see you've still got your sign, Mr. Earp. Your Last Kind Words sign," Nellie mentioned. "Were you planning on hanging it up anyplace around here?"

Warren, who had taken his hat off, immediately clapped it back on his head.

"We mean to get us a saloon in Arizona," Warren said. "Arizona has a fine climate—have you ever been?"

"Just to a dude ranch," Nellie told him. "Didn't care for the dude ranch much."

"Virg is sheriff of a place called Tombstone," Warren said. "Morg's his deputy. He says the thieves and murderers are too much for him. Guess we'll have to go help him and bring my sign."

"Tombstone's a mining town," Mary said. "They're usually rough."

Then Warren began to guzzle whiskey, from a bottle he had in the buggy.

Jessie had no way to stop him; she knew better than to come between an Earp and his bottle.

"Arizona," he said, to no one in particular, and then he slid slowly out of his chair and under the table.

"If I had a dollar for every man I've seen passed out drunk, I'd be rich," Nellie said.

Nobody disputed her claim. Jessie knew a few of her stars. On this occasion Venus shone bright in the west, while Jupiter was nearly as bright in the heaven straight above. Jessie thought it was mean of Wyatt to send her off with his brother. She was not convinced that there even was a place called Mobetie: unless it had a bar there'd be no place for her to work. But Wyatt and Doc just saddled up one day and rode off, but not before Wyatt borrowed fifty dollars from her.

"How you going to pay me back, Wyatt, you don't even have a job and it's still hundreds of miles to Arizona?"

Wyatt mounted up and rode off as if no one had spoken, taking the fifty dollars. He knew she was upset but he chose to ignore it. His view was not only that he got to borrow the fifty dollars but he shouldn't have to endure a discussion about it. So he didn't.

Jessie cried off and on all that day. Warren showed up eventually and drove the wagon over the endless plain.

·35·

Doc began to have long coughing jags, bringing up copious quantities of phlegm. Wyatt was a light sleeper at best. Doc's coughing always woke him and that would be the end of sleep for that particular night. The two of them had gone back to Long Grass because of the rail—which would route them here and there and maybe bring them to Arizona in a week or two.

On their trip back to Long Grass cattle were everywhere—there had been a big stampede. Doc was outraged. He had never been fond of cattle and could barely even tolerate horses.

"If the cowboys had been doing their job these plains would be empty."

"Yes, and then what would we eat if we were hungry?" Wyatt asked him.

"And I don't know why you're in such hurry to get to Arizona—it's just a place, and at the end of the day, most places present mostly the same problems."

"You have no optimism, Wyatt," Doc said. "We might break the bank in Arizona, if we can just get the cards to go our way."

He was holding back a cough, though.

"I won't lag around a pistol, though," Wyatt said. "A dern pistol's heavy on the hip."

"Jessie's a qualified bartender," Doc reminded him. "I bet she'd support you until you've got on your feet."

"No she won't, the hussy," Wyatt told him. "And she said she'd leave me if I tried to take any of her earnings."

"Do you ever wonder what it will be like to die?" Doc asked.

"No, I spend very little time in idle speculation," Wyatt said.

Then he had an idea.

Out back of what had once been called the Last Kind Words Saloon was a considerable dump, where the townspeople threw their trash; the dump was full of bottles and cans and other likely targets for rifle or pistol. What better time or place to practice.

"Let's go shoot," he said to Doc, who immediately drew his gun and whirled around. To his surprise the streets of Long Grass were empty.

"Shoot who?" he asked.

"No, no . . . not a cowboy or even a person, just shoot for practice, in case some show like Cody's comes along and hires us to do an act like we did in Denver."

Doc followed him around to the dump and watched him line up about thirty targets, mainly bottles and cans.

"This is a silly business," Doc said, but he allowed himself to be persuaded and was soon popping away at the various targets and missing most of them.

"Cody did mention that there were other shows like his."

Doc allowed himself to be persuaded, there being little else to do in Long Grass. Besides it was always fun to poke around in dumps and see what kinds of stuff human beings felt they could afford to throw away.

"Why here's a full bottle of hair lotion, somebody must have shot the barber," Doc said.

Wyatt found a solitary stirrup: no saddle, no cowboy, no horse, just a stirrup.

Doc sniffed the hair lotion and made a face. He threw the lotion back on the dump and shot at the bottle three times, missing clean.

"Whoever ordered that lotion probably got snake-bit and expired soon after," Doc said.

Wyatt didn't answer. Nine out of ten statements Doc made were nonsense, but it was dangerous to stop listening because the tenth statement might be really smart.

"Thirty bottles is enough," he said, once he had lined his thirty bottles on a low wall more or less behind the town. "The way to hit your target is to sight right down your arm and squeeze off a shot real slow."

He leveled his arm and sighted down his arm and squeezed off a shot very slowly. No bottles shattered.

"I have heard that the prone position is the more reliable when shooting Colt revolvers," Doc said.

He dropped to his knees but stopped there.

"There's cowshit everywhere here," he informed him. "I'll soil my vest if I lie prone."

Wyatt fired three times, shattering no bottles. Annoyed, he threw his pistol at the line of bottles, knocking over three. Then he took a derringer out of an inner pocket and shattered two, to his surprise.

Doc was still struggling with the difficult prone position. He shot but no bottles shattered. He drew back his arm to throw the gun but then caught himself at the last second.

"Throwing guns is a bad habit," he said. "You might throw your gun away just as some loose Indians come charging down upon you."

"There ain't no more loose Indians, Doc," Wyatt said. "But if there were, throwing your gun wouldn't help you."

He fired once more with the derringer and shattered a bottle.

"Good lord, I hit one," he said. "Luck ain't to be despised."

"Who said I despised it?" Doc said, dusting off his vest.

·36·

Later Doc paid a visit to the barbershop, which was also the blacksmith shop. The barber, a wizened little fellow named Red, was also the blacksmith. He'd be shoeing horses one minute and shaving whiskers the next.

"Somebody threw away a bottle of hair lotion," Doc said. "It's over in the dump, about two-thirds full. I hate to see such a fine product go to waste."

"Oh it came from Scotland," Red said. "It belonged to one of them bagpipers."

"If Scotland's that smelly I believe I'll give it a pass. I will take a shave and try not to cut my throat."

"Shouldn't tempt me," Red said. "Only I can't afford to cut nobody's throat. There's few enough customers in this town anyway."

Later in the day Doc heard the same sentiment from an

aging whore named Edna, his favorite local whore. She still worked out of the Orchid Hotel, which had grown shabby since San Saba left. The famous Twelve Inches Free sign had been dusted over. Edna's breasts had fallen and she smoked cheroots but she was tolerant of Doc's coughing and she had a fine sense of humor—often she giggled a girlish giggle, which Doc liked to hear. He liked her so much that he asked her about that famous local sign—the man with a twelve-inch member gets to visit free. Doc had always figured the twelve inches was just a joke, but when he brought it up with Edna she giggled and looked coy.

"I doubt there's a man alive with a dick that long," he said.

"You ain't a whore, Doc," Edna said. "It ain't common but it ain't unheard of, either. Now and then a cowpoke will walk in with a thing on him you wouldn't believe."

"What do you do when that happens?"

Edna shrugged. "Same as we do for anybody, only it's free."

Doc looked around the shabby room—there was dust on the pillows.

"What'll you do when this place shuts down?"

Edna shrugged. "Go back to some place where they don't know me. Pennsylvania, maybe."

Doc felt it unlikely, but Edna looked hopeful. Why shatter a dream?

·37·

It was two weeks after the big stampede, and Charlie
Goodnight had been home only twice—if it *was* his home—
and Mary Goodnight had stopped being worried and began to
be annoyed.

"I guess Charlie would rather work than be married," Mary
said. "The way I see it he'd rather work than do anything."

"Many men would rather work than be married," San Saba
said. "Your husband is not abnormal in that respect."

"That's true of my husband," Nellie put in. "Zenas would
throw any ball that's handed to him."

Then they saw a rider coming from the north, though not
coming very rapidly.

"Is that fellow riding a mule?" Mary asked.

"He is," San Saba said. "In fact I know him: it's Russell of
the *Times*."

"That's right," Nellie said. "I remember him now. I wonder

where he found the mule, and why he'd want it, anyway. He's the most famous journalist in the world. It's rumored that the Queen intends to knight him someday."

"That's very unlikely," Russell said. "Queen Victoria has a lot to do—she needn't start giving knighthood to hacks like yours truly."

He dismounted and Mary Goodnight gave him a forthright handshake, which he took.

"I apologize for my husband," Mary said. "I suppose he's off sorting cattle."

"He is," Russell said. "Yesterday I met a Mr. Pierce, who's at the same task. And I understand there's a Mr. Wagoner, whom I have not met."

"I hope to see your husband tomorrow," he said.

"Why?" Mary said. "If he's in a bad mood, as I suspect he is, then he'll hardly be worth seeing."

"I was hoping he'd show me the place where Lord Ernle died," Russell said. "I've been asked by the family to do a short book about him."

"Goodness, do you write books too?"

"Trifles, yes," Russell said. "I'm quick though. I should be able to do the career of Lord Benny Ernle in about two weeks."

"Who would want to read it?" Nellie asked. "The man was a fool, else he'd be alive."

Howard Russell was amused. The unschooled American lady had posed a good question. Who would want to read about the late Lord Ernle, clearly a very rich but very foolish man.

"I'm surprised to find you here, Madame Saba," he said. "I had supposed you'd want to go home."

San Saba nodded her head.

"It's a fine question, where my home is, Mr. Russell," she said. "I was raised in Turkey but I'm sure not going back there, after what happened to my mother."

"I recall some irregularities about your mother—the Rose Concubine. I met Sultan Hamid once. Nothing nice about him that I recall," he said.

"I wonder where the eunuchs went?" he asked.

"To hell, I hope," San Saba said.

A great red sun was just then setting to the west. In the sky the planet Venus shone brightly.

"I customarily enjoy a brandy at this hour," he said. "I've a bottle in my saddlebags. Would you ladies care to imbibe?"

San Saba declined. She had never cared for brandy, or, indeed, for anything stronger than beer.

But Mary and Nellie *did* care to imbibe. After all they were married, and yet where were their husbands?

"If there was a band we could dance," Mary said. She went to every dance she could find, though getting Charlie Goodnight on a dance floor was seldom worth the effort. But, somewhere in the crowd, there was usually a cowboy who wasn't afraid to dance with his boss's wife.

Nellie danced a few steps by herself. The prairie winds sighed through what was left of Lord Ernle's great house.

Russell of the *Times* found Mary Goodnight very appealing. He offered her his arm and she took it.

"We could hum, Mr. Russell," Mary said; and so they did, while Nellie Courtright danced alone.

·38·

Goodnight was impatient when the English-man on the mule showed up, wanting to see where Lord Ernle had gone off the cut bank. The sorting of the three herds had not gone well, which was only to be expected since there was some eight thousand cattle. Goodnight's brand book was some help, but the other two cattlemen had lost theirs; besides which many of the original brands had been grown over or blurred.

The sorting took more than ten days, and left none of the original owners fully satisfied.

"Hazards of the business, I guess," Russell said. "Force majeure, I suppose."

"No sir, it was bad planning on my part," Goodnight said. "Next time I start I'll be sure to have these damn plains to myself."

"I wonder what the longitude is," Russell said, startling Goodnight.

"Why would you care about the longitude?" Goodnight wondered. "Lord Ernle is dead, whatever the longitude."

Russell ignored the rebuke.

"I want to compliment you on your excellent wife," he added. "You don't often see a woman that spirited this far out on the veldt."

"I heard you danced with her—what did you do for music?"

"I whistled some and we hummed. A swallow or two of brandy was enough to limber us up," Russell said.

Goodnight looked at the man closely, trying to see them in his mind's eye. He had only meant to be gone a week, but the sorting dragged on and was imperfect anyway.

I better get home, he thought. Mary sounds mad.

The Englishman pulled a large album out of his saddlebag and began to sketch.

Why does the fellow bother, Goodnight thought. There's nothing to see but a bleak bend of the Canadian River. But when he showed the sketch to Goodnight the cattleman was impressed.

"Dern, you've got the gift, sir—you even got in that little hawk up there soaring."

"I like to have a record, even if I have to do the drawing myself," Russell said.

·39·

Mary was a little huffy next time Charlie got home, but she cooked him a beefsteak anyway. Nellie Courtright had just gone home.

"She made friends with Shanghai Pierce—Nellie could make friends with anybody," Mary added.

It was Charlie's turn to get huffy.

"Well, I don't approve," he said.

"Don't approve of what? Nellie needed to get home and Shanghai was going that way."

"I have a low opinion of Shanghai Pierce," he said. For some reason it rankled him that Nellie had gone off with the man—a loudmouth and a braggart, in his opinion.

"You have a low opinion of everybody, Charlie," Mary said. "Except Bose: he's the only one that qualifies."

"No, you qualify," he said. "Would I have married someone I didn't approve of?"

"It's not a question I can answer," Mary said. "I've often wondered why you married me—and I wonder even more why I married you."

He looked across the table and saw San Saba smiling. She said little, but Mary had already told him that she had been a big help with school, and several cowboys mentioned that she had also improved the mustangs. It seemed to him that he and Mary were accumulating a pretty unusual household, but so far it wasn't a bad thing.

At the moment he couldn't get his mind off Nellie Courtright, whose husband Zenas was somewhere in the South Seas. There was no knowing if Zenas was even alive, or if he would come back—meanwhile there was Nellie, a comely woman if there ever was one.

Goodnight considered Nellie to be both impudent and rash, like all women, and yet he thought of her often: more often, probably, than he spent thinking about his own admirable wife, who certainly paid close attention to his behavior. He considered himself a man of certainties. He meant to speak to Mary about her constant scrutiny but every time he got ready to say something Mary got some comment in first. It made him wonder why he talked to Mary at all, since in most conversations he came away feeling like a fool.

Later, while they were eating cobbler San Saba made with some peaches she found somewhere, Mary suddenly guffawed.

"Why, I've got it: this big oaf has got the sweets for Nellie. Think he'll run off with her, folks?"

The table consisted of herself, Charlie, San Saba, Flo, and Caddo Jake, who came by to give Mary some fossils he had found. His was a fragrant presence thanks to the skunks, but Mary liked the old man and never sent him away.

"Company's too scarce out here on the baldies," Mary said. "I can't afford to be picky."

Caddo Jake took no interest in the Goodnights' domestic life, and neither did San Saba and Flo.

"You couldn't talk such bosh in front of the company," Charlie told Mary. "I have known Nellie Courtright a damn long time and I take some interest in her welfare, that's all, and traveling with Shanghai Pierce is risky at best."

Mary was smiling to herself, a habit he deplored. If something was funny why not speak out? And if it wasn't funny, why not keep quiet?

Caddo Jake soon nodded off; Mary passed the cobbler to Charlie, who always liked peaches. He awarded himself a goodly serving.

The west wind blew through the ruin of Lord Ernle's great house. It was picking up force and Mary felt it and felt a moment's alarm. A huge red sun was sinking in the west: then the sun vanished and darkness came.

Goodnight had been on the plains in all weathers but had never seen the sun go so quickly.

Caddo Jake snapped awake and looked to the west.

"Sand," he said, and that was all he said.

·40·

The sand came like a wall—a moving wall one hundred feet high. Seeing it come, Jessie felt an overpowering fear. They were in a train just west of Deming, New Mexico, which was not much of a town. Wyatt and Doc had spent most of the night in saloons there and she had stayed with them out of fear. There was a parrot and the parrot kept saying Joe. Wyatt didn't like her staying in bars unless she was working and she wasn't working. They were on their way to Arizona, where he promised her she could get a job tending bar.

Now Wyatt and Doc were looking at the wall of sand with amazement: so were the few passengers on the train.

"My lord, what's that?" Doc said: he was startled but not particularly alarmed. Neither was Wyatt alarmed, though the wall of sand dwarfed the train.

"What do you think, Doc? Can a wall of sand push over a train?"

"Hope not," Doc said, and then pitch darkness came.

"Hope not too," Wyatt said. Jessie buried her face in Wyatt's chest. Suddenly it was pitch dark. Sand began to seep into the car through the doors and windows. Jessie began to feel grit on her teeth. The door to the car they were in didn't fit quite snug. Big tumbleweeds blowing from the north began to smack into the wall, which annoyed Doc.

"Jessie's upset," Wyatt said. "She's shaking like a leaf, and she ain't a leaf."

He was just remembering how aggravating it was to travel with a woman, particularly Jessie.

And when Jessie wasn't scared she was mad.

"We're in a pickle, we're in a pickle," he said, three or four times. Only a minute before the moon had been shining brightly. He stood at the back of the train, smoking a cheroot. For some reason Jessie didn't like the smell of tobacco—even fine tobacco—so when it wasn't chilly he went outside to smoke. Now it was blowing so hard he didn't dare step out. He might blow right off the train and be lost in New Mexico—if they were still even in New Mexico.

One windowpane was broken in their car and the sand poured in as if it were being pumped.

"Hush, goddamnit," Wyatt said.

"It won't kill us. It'll blow over directly."

"What if it doesn't?" Jessie said. "What if God sent it to punish us for our sins."

The comment struck Doc as funny. He slapped his leg and laughed, which brought him a glare from Wyatt, although he didn't see it. Wyatt's sense of humor was limited at times.

Then the car began to rock from the force of the wind. It would rock and settle back, rock and settle back.

In Doc's memory no railroad car had ever rocked that way.

They had brought no horses. If the train blew over they would have to make it about thirty miles back to Deming, New Mexico. It would be a hard straggle.

Then a whole window blew in and sand followed until they were up to their knees in it. Jessie sobbed hopelessly.

"I would never have considered Arizona if I had known it was going to be so goddamn dusty," Wyatt said.

Jessie began to pray to the saints. "Oh, Saint Michael," she praised. "Oh, Saint George."

"A woman who just keeps talking when the menfolks would rather have quiet is a woman who's asking for trouble," Wyatt said.

It angered Jessie slightly. She reached in her bag and came out with a pocketknife, which she opened with her teeth, and pointed it at Wyatt, who had just managed to get a lantern lit. He didn't like the look in Jessie's eye.

"What were you going to do, Wyatt, cut my throat?" she asked. Her eyes flashed in a way that Wyatt didn't like.

"I merely meant to shake you, put away that knife," Wyatt said. If the knife impressed him he didn't show it.

"You may not mean business but I do," Jessie said. "You oughtn't to have brought me to a place this terrible."

"You don't know," he said. "This train might be headed straight to paradise."

Jessie stood her ground, the hot look in her eye.

"Put that darn knife down before I'm forced to shoot you," Wyatt said.

Wyatt didn't shoot her.

After a time he went to the back of the car and lit a cheroot.

·41·

"The children just like the guts," Quanah said. He sat next to Goodnight, watching the butchery going on below them. In the great sandstorm that no plains person would ever forget, Goodnight's herd had run before it so near the Palo Duro rim that eighteen animals had been pushed off a cutback to their doom. All of them broke at least one limb. These Goodnight shot and the Indian children were pulling out the guts and eating them like candy. Occasionally an aggressive dog would snatch a piece. Several old Comanche women were cutting out the sweetbreads, while others set up poles on which to dry the meat.

"It's not only Englishmen who can run off cliffs," Goodnight said. "We're about one hundred miles from your reservation. How did you happen to hear about it so quick?"

"The birds told us, and the wolves—especially the wolves," Quanah said. "There's two of them right now."

Sure enough, two lobo wolves were watching the operation.

"They hope to get the bones," Quanah explained.

"I've seen wolves before," Goodnight said. "What did you do when the big sandstorm hit?"

"Went to a cellar," Quanah said. "All but one woman, and that one was pretty dusty. We found her in a ditch when morning came."

"Surely this mansion had a cellar," he added.

"Nope, but I aim to start digging one tomorrow," he said, swinging in the saddle.

"Thank you for the beef," Quanah said.

"A dead beef animal is no use to me," Goodnight said. "The lesson here if there is one is that I need to do my ranching on the flatland prairie. No dern cutbacks."

"I'm glad you and I didn't have to fight. I can beat most white men, but you're quick."

"I hear you once could have taken Mackenzie's scalp," Goodnight replied, referring to the brilliant young cavalry officer who did more than any American soldier to break the Comanche power on the south plains.

"Yes, at Blanco Canyon, before he learned how to fight us," Quanah said. "But he learned how to fight us and he fought us only too well."

"So why'd you spare him, Quanah?"

Quanah shrugged.

"For no reason," he said. "Sometimes I just do things like that. Then, later on, he beat us good, and he even beat Dull Knife too."

Goodnight watched the Indian children eating gut.

"You went in but you didn't always stay in," Goodnight said. "I'd still like to know how you found out about these eighteen beeves."

"Just gossip," Quanah said. "Caddo Jake knew about it."

"They say Mackenzie went crazy the night before his wedding and he died in New York in an asylum," Goodnight said.

"Yes, we fought him too hard," Quanah said.

"I rarely talk this much in a week," Goodnight said, and rode away.

· 42 ·

When Goodnight was out of sight one of the old
Comanche women who was drying beef began to badger
Quanah. Her name was Crow Talks and she talked as much
as any crow. Her incessant chatter annoyed most warriors but
Quanah indulged her and didn't beat her. The main reason for
his forebearance was that she had been a friend of his mother,
Cynthia Ann. He had a hunger for news of his mother, even
though she was dead.

Crow Talks knew of his longing and told him many stories,
including some that weren't true.

"Goodnight was there when the whites took your mother
back," Crow Talks said.

"Yes . . . you tell me that every time I see you," he said.

"You should have killed him," she said.

"If I had, whose beef would we be eating now?"

"Nobody's beef," he added. Sometimes he answered his own questions.

"There are lots of stories now about the old days . . . the time of the People," the old woman said. "I'm a forgetful old woman . . . myself. I have never been quite sure what happened to your father, Peta."

"Peta was wounded in the Palo Duro fight, when Mackenzie beat us," Quanah said, wondering why he bothered to talk to this pesky old woman. Maybe it was because he liked to be reminded of the years of the Comanche glory, when the People were lords of the plain—then they could go anywhere, kill anybody, torture and scalp.

"I was not in that battle," Crow Talks said.

"No woman was in that battle," he reminded her, with a sharp look.

"Peta was good to your mother," she said, thinking it might be time to change the subject.

Quanah had been with his father as the wound from Mackenzie's soldiers festered and pulled Peta away.

They were picking wild plums on the Canadian River when it happened. Eight warriors sang over him as he died.

Peta had been their leader; at his death Quanah became the leader. Not all Comanches were pleased with that, but none challenged him, not even Isatai, the medicine man who had failed so badly when, for a second time, they tried to drive the buffalo hunters out of the old trading post called Adobe Walls.

The whites had attacked there once before, led by the great Kit Carson, but the People had been strong then and Carson had barely escaped with his life.

In the second battle, when Isatai assured them that his magic was unbeatable, it had not proved as unbeatable as the big .50 caliber Spencer rifles, guns that could kill at a mile's distance. Isatai lost his power then. He tried to blame his defeat on a skunk, but all the warriors knew it was caused by those Spencer rifles.

Crow Talks started in on something but Quanah cut her off.

"I don't want that beef to spoil," he said. "Go back to your work."

·43·

Wyatt, Doc, and Jessie entered Arizona by way of Lordsburg, New Mexico. The sandstorm that cost Charles Goodnight eighteen cattle also gummed up several cars on the Southern Pacific Railroad.

The coach that finally carried them west also contained a fat woman with three howling brats and a Frenchman who spoke no English.

Naturally the coach rattled and bounced. Doc picked up a toothache and Jessie grew queasy from the uneven progress. Wyatt was merely bored.

"I didn't bargain for cactus," Jessie said.

"Well, you got some, bargain or not," Wyatt replied. He tried to remember a time when Jessie had sounded friendly, but he couldn't think of one.

"I hope I don't have to pull my own tooth," Doc said. "What a tragedy that would be."

Just at that moment the fat woman came out with a scream.

"I seen an Indian," she said. Her three brats howled with her.

Wyatt glanced out the window and sure enough there was an Indian, a short brown man with a Winchester standing by a yucca that was taller than himself.

"She's right," Wyatt informed the company. "There's an Indian fellow out by that yucca."

"I don't suppose a naked savage would be able to afford dental work," Doc said.

He had a strong urge to throw the three howling brats out the window, but refrained.

"I wonder if Virg and Warren have got their saloon open yet," Wyatt mentioned. "I would welcome a few swallows of whiskey."

"You promised me I could bartend," Jessie reminded him. "It's my main pleasure."

"You can bartend if there's a bar," Wyatt assured her. "I'll be the bouncer, if one's needed."

"Unless we get scalped in the next few miles," he added.

"What's that?" Doc asked. "I was reliably informed that all the wild Indians had run off to Mexico."

"You may not be as reliably informed as you like to think," Wyatt said. "The one I just saw wasn't in Mexico. For all I know it was Geronimo himself. He was carrying a Winchester rifle, which is an expensive gun."

Ahead they saw a cluster of shacks, which seemed to be all the Arizona towns consisted of. Jessie was getting the feeling that she had made a mistake leaving Kansas City.

"That's probably Tombstone," Wyatt said.

But it wasn't. It was Douglas, a town on the border. But any chance to stretch their legs was welcome. No sooner had the three brats hit the ground than they took off running, at which point their mother started praying to the angels. Then one of the engineers began to beat on another.

"Let them scuffle," Doc said. "Fisticuffs will often clear the brain."

"Get my boys, get 'em," the desperate fat woman said.

"Where are we, Wyatt?" Jessie asked. "I thought there'd be lots of buildings."

"I don't know about the lots of buildings," Wyatt said. "You know how Virg exaggerates when he's drunk."

"Which is often," Doc said.

"You mind your own business," Wyatt said, snappishly. He did not like to hear any of his brothers criticized, unless it was by him.

Doc ignored this threat and walked over to the two Butter-field men who had been exchanging blows. His hope was that a tooth or two might have been knocked loose. In fact when he arrived both men were spitting out teeth.

"I'm a practitioner of the dental arts," he said. "Either of you gents need attention?"

"We were bound for Tombstone, but some ignorant fool forgot to pull the main switch and here we are in Douglas."

Jessie could not remember feeling as lost as she felt at that moment. There was still probably a fine haze of dust in the air. There had been that Indian by the yucca. Doc had often explained to her what a fine scalp her long lustrous hair would make.

Wyatt was studying a little pocket map he had bought in Chicago a while back. He had found an empty bucket somewhere and sat on it while he read his map.

"Tombstone ain't such a far piece from here," he said.

"It wouldn't be if we had firewood enough," the engineer said. "But we missed the big wood yard in that sandstorm," the man said. "And now we're short of fuel."

"It's times like these when a deck of cards comes in handy— and I happen to have a deck of cards."

Suddenly a high whirling dust devil came racing up the street. Jessie wanted to run but where was there to run? The small Frenchman had just stepped out of the train, just in time to walk right into it, which snatched his hat and blew it high in the sky. Fortunately the dust devil quickly dissolved.

"That dude picked the wrong time to get off the train," Doc said.

No one disagreed.

Jessie got back on the train and had a cry.

·44·

"Miguel throws the prettiest loop of any vaquero I've ever seen," Goodnight said to San Saba. They were watching a team of six cowboys castrate some long yearlings that should have been cut months before. The vaquero Goodnight was praising was neither a young man nor a large man, but his skill with the lariat exceeded anything she had ever seen.

"Yes, quite a pretty loop," San Saba said. In her time with Goodnight she had acquired some roping skills herself, but her roping did not compare with Miguel's.

Goodnight, who rarely praised anyone, could not heap praise enough on Miguel.

"And it ain't just his roping," Goodnight went on. "He's the best trail boss I know, and I'm pretty good with a trail myself. But Miguel will pick up a herd of three thousand and let them graze along and not lose a head—and most of them will weigh more in Kansas than they weighed in Texas. I've not the patience for that kind of driving. I push, and that's asking for trouble."

"You do push, Mr. Goodnight," San Saba told him. "And for some reason you're still nervous about me. I don't know why."

"I don't either," Goodnight admitted. "I suppose I've not had your opportunities. I know cattle and not much else."

"How about your wife . . . there's a lot to know there," she said.

"Mary's a force of nature and I've only one lifetime to learn about her."

In the lots Miguel made a particularly difficult throw. The yearling went down and the cowboys were on him.

Miguel flashed a look and San Saba returned it. Goodnight saw the look but let it pass. He didn't ask.

"I confess I've grown fond of Miguel, Mr. Goodnight," she said. "He makes wonderful snares and gives me what he catches: prairie chickens, sometimes a quail. Mary and I and Flo often lunch on what Miguel snares."

"I could probably eat a prairie chicken, if I was offered one," Goodnight said.

"Maybe Mary will ask you to lunch," she said. "Then you'll be back to get another trail herd and we ladies will be back to beefsteak."

"Miguel has a wife and thirteen children—did you know that, Mr. Goodnight?" she asked.

"I didn't," Goodnight admitted. "When I need Miguel I go to San Antonio and send for him. So far he's always come."

"Thirteen is a passel of children," he said. "Maybe he likes to get away from them. I would."

"Maybe, but mainly he comes for me," she said. "We're having a little romance. A very light one, no threats to the rest of our arrangements. There's just a smile, like the one today. Just a smile, now and then. That's as far as I care to go, romantically."

Goodnight searched his mind for a reply, couldn't find one— so he tipped his hat politely and walked off.

It stuck in his mind through supper, or dinner as the women came to call it. He mentioned it to Mary as she was getting ready for bed. She had her gown in her hand and held it in front of her while she looked at him.

"Did Saba tell you that or did you finally notice?"

"Notice what—I mainly just complimented his roping."

With women it didn't take long for things to slip out of kilter.

"I mainly just said what a good trail boss he was."

"You managed to miss the main point, Charlie," she said.

"I don't have even a notion but I'm sure you're going to tell me what the main point is," he said. "I'll just await the news."

"Miguel's in love with San Saba, that's plain as the nose on your face," Mary said just as she blew out the lantern—after which she pulled down her gown.

"Good lord," Goodnight said. "He lives in the brush country, which is a damn long way from here. He only gets this way when I hire him to bring a herd—maybe twice a year. If he wants to snare prairie chickens and give them to San Saba, that's fine with me."

"How it would sit with his wife is another question, but she's a long way off. I hear that he's got a passel of kids."

"They're chaste in their ways of course," she said. But when he reached for her hand she directed it to a wet place—it was clear she herself was not at the moment feeling chaste.

"That's not all the news," Mary said, when they were resting. "San Saba's leaving us; she's moving to Paris, France."

At that Goodnight sat up. "Paris, France," he said. "Why would she do that, when she's just about got my horses gentle enough to ride?"

"She doesn't like the plains and I can't blame her. Too somber," Mary said. "A count asked her to come—he's the richest man in France, except for the Rothschilds. You've heard of them, I guess."

"I haven't but they're probably bankers," he said.

"Maybe we can visit France, someday."

"Mary, we can barely pay the hands," he said.

Then he noticed that Mary was crying; her face was wet.

Before he could move she swatted him with a pillow.

"Shut up, Charlie," she said. "Every word you utter just makes it worse."

Charles Goodnight shut up.

·45·

The Goodnights accompanied San Saba and Flo
back to Long Grass, to see them off. Goodnight drove the
buggy himself. The three women were sad.

"I think the thing I dislike most about America is the lack of
trees."

"Oh, there are some, just not around here," Mary said. "I
know what you mean about missing them, though. These bare
plains are just too sad."

"I'm sorry you ladies don't like the plains—I'm a cattleman
and I need to operate where there's an abundance of edible
grass."

They had asked Miguel to come with them but he merely
tipped his hat politely and turned away. What was there to say?

News of San Saba's departure traveled far and wide in the
plains country. Nellie Courtright, still more or less a widow,
came racing down the plains, hoping to get a story.

San Saba had come to like Nellie and helped her out this time.

"You still can't call me a madam, though," San Saba said.

"Then what *can* I call you?" Nellie asked.

"Just call me a consort—a consort is a kind of companion to rich and titled men. Right now it's Count Erlander who'll be keeping me."

"How do you spell that—and what does he do?" Nellie asked.

San Saba laughed.

"The men who keep me don't do anything," she said. "I think he broke the bank at Monte Carlo once—and I believe he likes the races. That's what he does."

Goodnight was glad the mood had lightened. Driving a buggy with three women in it was no light task, and Long Grass, when they got there, did not seem to be thriving. Only one saloon was open and the livery stable seemed to be on its last legs. Fortunately Bose had come with them to take care of the team.

"The last time I rode into this town it was full of Earps. I have no liking for Earps, nor for that dentist who rides with them."

"Yes, Doc Holliday," Nellie said. "He's often rude, though a good shot nonetheless."

"How would you know how good a shot he is?" he inquired.

"Because I work for newspapers now and they like stories about gunfighters. I won't work for the Denver paper though, because of what Harry Tammen did to Bill Cody—sold his show right out from under him. I loved Bill Cody and will never forgive Harry Tammen."

"I'm glad you're loyal," he said.

"I don't see any Earps here," he said.

"No, you'll find them in Arizona," Nellie said. "They've taken over a place called Tombstone. Virgil Earp's the sheriff and Warren Earp runs the biggest saloon. I don't know what Wyatt does, you'll have to ask him yourself."

"I've heard of Tombstone," Goodnight said. "There's an old ruffian named Clanton who makes his living stealing Mexican cattle. He tried to sell me some once but I declined—Mexican cattle often have the fevers."

"So I've heard," Nellie said.

"The Earps had better watch close," Goodnight said. "Old Man Clanton is a murderer as well as a thief. He ought to have been hung long ago but so far nobody's been up to the task. I know there's a multitude of Earps but most of them can't shoot and Clanton's got an army, some of whom *can* shoot."

"Well, I'm not the mother, but when I get home I might send Warren a message—maybe write him a letter, warning them about Old Man Clanton. I might even do a story on them, if they'd allow it."

"I think you yourself have more of a story but I somehow doubt that you'd invite me to write it up."

"You're correct, I wouldn't. Where's the story in driving cattle?"

"Don't waste your time on him," Mary said. "Half the time he won't even tell me what he wants for breakfast."

While the Goodnights bickered Flo and San Saba walked across to the place that had been the Orchid. Goodnight hired a young cowboy named Teddy Blue, who was known to be knowledgable about Montana, a range Goodnight had been keeping his eye on—he was thinking of expanding there, once he got his panhandle operation the way he wanted it.

San Saba walked through the house she had once ruled.

"Benny Ernle could have sent me to a lot of places," she said. "I wonder why he sent me here. Seems like he wanted to see me on a ranch."

"Life is full of surprises, isn't it, Flo?" she said.

Flo didn't say. Her main hope was never to leave San Saba. Without her Flo knew she wouldn't last long.

In the morning, just as they were boarding the train a fierce hailstorm swept the plains. In three minutes the whole prairie was white with hail. Flo and San Saba were safe in the sturdy railroad car and the Goodnights and Nellie took refuge in the livery stable.

Five miles or so from Long Grass the hail stopped and the sun shone brightly.

"I'll just bet you're going to like Paris," San Saba said. "Honey, I just bet you will."

Then they heard a whoop and there was that cowboy, Teddy Blue, waving his hat and racing the train.

"That's fine of him, let's blow him a kiss," San Saba said. She and Flo waved and blew him kisses until the cowboy slowly fell behind.

· 46 ·

Goodnight was vexed by the hailstorm: he resented any delay. Lately it seemed he was mostly doing chores for women—chores for which he was largely unfitted. Mary wanted a grape arbor, for example, and she also wanted a proper outhouse: Lord Ernle had not gotten around to installing proper plumbing in his mansion.

If it wasn't one thing it was another. Every few miles she produced a fresh set of tears: missing her friend, he supposed. He thought about asking her what was the matter, but even the simplest question might preface a fresh tear burst.

"Is there anyone in this world that you'd miss, Charlie?" she asked once.

"You, maybe," he said. "Or if I needed some reliable roping done I might miss Miguel."

"Yes, you're a practical man," she said.

"If I weren't practical where would we be?" he asked.

"I don't know where you'd be, mister," she said. "Probably looking at the back end of a cow."

"That's the likely thing," he said, refraining from asking where she'd be: that was too big a question to tie into.

TOMBSTONE

·47·

Doc's health was failing: most days he just sat in the sun, of which, usually, there was an abundance in southern Arizona. He spat frequently, and dosed himself with morphine saved up from dental operations, what few there were; they took place in the Last Kind Words Saloon, itself still run by Warren Earp, with Jessie still the bartender.

Wyatt was not often seen, thanks to his dislike of drinking in saloons where his lovely wife worked behind the bar. Jessie, though, thrived in her job.

"I need gamblers and whores and plenty of drunks to keep me perking," Jessie once said to Doc. She liked her job and didn't care that Wyatt, her husband, frequented the bar up the street.

When he did drift down to the Last Kind Words he mainly sat with Doc, trying to come up with ways to get rich without really working.

"I've got plenty of brothers who can work," Wyatt said. "Virgil and Morgan constitute what there is of a police force here. I see no reason to burden myself with marshaling, though of course if some drunk gets too disorderly I might lend a hand."

Doc was of the opinion that Wyatt was too cavalier about the prospect of sudden gunplay.

"There's enough weaponry in this town to outfit the Union army. And yet you walk around unarmed, although you have plenty of enemies."

"Oh, just the Clantons, I suppose you mean," Wyatt said. "I reckon I can handle the Clantons and that riffraff if I need to."

"Unarmed?" Doc asked.

"No, of course not," Wyatt said. "Wells Fargo keeps a shotgun ready, which I've been able to borrow from time to time."

"I've heard that Johnny-Behind-the-Deuce works for Old Man Clanton now," Doc said. "And there's the McLaury brothers, and Curly Bob Brocious and Johnny Ringo and a few more."

"Shucks," Wyatt said. "Most of those fellows live a hundred miles away. I could have a war and finish it before they could even get here."

"Maybe, but I still think a pistol would be a reasonable precaution."

But Wyatt had become bored with the topic and gone into the saloon to have a word with Jessie, who happened to be deep in conversation with the last man mentioned, Johnny Ringo.

The two men had not met before.

"Hello, I'm Wyatt," Wyatt said.

"Hello, I'm Johnny," Ringo said, shaking hands. He wore an expensive hat, and sported a thin mustache.

"What did you want, Wyatt, Johnny and I were talking," Jessie said.

"Now that you put it that way, nothing," Wyatt said; he immediately walked out.

"Why didn't you tell me that damn outlaw was courting my wife?"

"Courting, oh come now," Doc said, and spat. "He reads, you know," Doc added. "He can quote; Shakespeare and all sorts of poets."

Wyatt in fact had known that Johnny Ringo had literary inclinations.

It didn't raise his opinion of Ringo by much.

"He won't be spouting it for me," Wyatt said, frowning as hard as he could frown.

"If he ain't careful I'll throw him off this porch," he added, looking hot.

·48·

As soon as Jessie stepped into their room Wyatt uncurled himself out of a chair and punched her full in the face, knocking her almost across the bed and splitting her lip, which bled profusely on her new blouse. It also made her head ring: Wyatt had never hit her with his closed fist before.

But she had been expecting it. She was the bartender and she was supposed to be nice to customers, who paid good money for their drinks—unlike Wyatt, who seldom paid for his drinks. He'd get a dude to pay for them, and allow the dude to have his picture made with the great Wyatt Earp.

Jessie had a derringer in her bag but before she could level it Wyatt yanked it away from her and gave her a hard slap.

"That's twice you hit me, you cowardly son of a bitch," Jessie said. "Do it once more and I'm gone."

She saw that Wyatt was trembling; in a minute he would start crying, and that's exactly what he did.

"Oh Jessie, why will you provoke me? I don't mean to hit you—it just wells over."

He came to the bed and tried to embrace her, but she rolled off on the other side.

"Leave me alone—go find a whore," Jessie said.

"I'll go, but don't you be talking to Johnny Ringo," Wyatt said.

"He was just a customer—I was showing him how to make a gimlet," she said. "I work for your brother Warren, remember? He don't want me sulking behind the bar."

"Nobody cares what that fool wants," Wyatt said, and left.

It took a while for Jessie's busted lip to stop bleeding; also her face began to puff up. Tomorrow she would be black and blue.

Maybe I can tell folks I fell off a wagon, she thought.

·49·

Warren Earp was meticulous about the upkeep of his gambling establishment, the Last Kind Words Saloon. It didn't rain much in Tombstone but when it did rain it poured, which is why Warren and his brother Virgil were up on the roof, patching a few leaks, and thus were the first to see the big dust cloud coming from down Sonora way—or the Clanton way, as you preferred. It probably meant that Old Man Clanton was coming through with a big herd of skinny Mexican cattle.

"Here he comes with a herd," the roofers yelled, before scampering down.

Wyatt and Doc were having breakfast on the porch of the saloon; the prospect of having their eggs covered with a lot of Mexican dust did not please them.

In fact all over Tombstone citizens were slamming windows

shut, ripping laundry off clotheslines, quickly stabling horses, or in general trying to prepare in a few minutes to meet the tower of dust created by nine hundred cattle as they passed through a town that was dusty anyway.

"Why the old bastard; just when I was enjoying my eggs," Doc said.

"That old fool . . . has he still got that big lead steer?" Wyatt asked.

"Old Monte . . . I believe so," Doc said, referring to a great red ox that Old Man Clanton had acquired somewhere; Monte had a calming effect on the nervous Mexican cattle that he dealt in.

"By god he's coming straight through," Doc added.

"We'll see about that," Wyatt said. He carefully set his breakfast on the porch, stepped quickly into the saloon and returned with a lariat and a .44 pistol, the latter stuck casually under his belt.

"Uh-oh, Mr. Earp is swinging into action," Doc said. "Do I need to borrow a firearm on this bright morning?"

"Don't bother," Wyatt said.

He stepped into the middle of the street and waited. There were six vaqueros driving the cattle—when they saw Wyatt blocking their way they fell silent and looked around anxiously for whatever support the Clantons intended to give.

To the south, about a mile away, several cowboys—or riders at least—trotted along on the upwind side of the herd, obviously to avoid the dust, which was thick. They had not noticed Wyatt and didn't seem to be looking for trouble.

"What are you up to, Wyatt?" Doc asked. "There is no reason to stir up the Clantons and their damn gunhands."

"You wasn't always so damn timid," Wyatt said, his eye on the great red ox, which was coming peaceably toward him, watched by half the citizens of Tombstone, from whatever vantage points they could secure.

"Whoa, Monte," Wyatt said. He gave the big steer a little tap on his nose with the coiled-up lariat, at which point Monte stopped. And, when Monte stopped, so did the Clanton herd, vaqueros and all.

Wyatt reached out and stroked Monte's nose.

"I guess we've got us an impasse," he said.

"An impasse and after that a coffin—I doubt the Clantons will think kindly of your impasse."

Wyatt just smiled and stepped back onto the porch, and Monte made no move to go on.

He looked around quizzically and stood where he was, placidly chewing his cud.

"Monte would make a good pet, though expensive to feed," Wyatt observed.

Doc was looking at the riders to the south, one of whom had detached himself from the group and was heading for Tombstone at a high lope. The other riders stayed where they were.

Jessie stepped out of the saloon, hoping to see what was happening, but Wyatt immediately waved her back in. The two of them were getting along a little better; Jesse didn't want to stir him up.

Doc felt more and more nervous.

"I don't like this," he said, and then he said it again.

"It's my play, Doc . . . you can leave if you don't like it," Wyatt said. "Just sidle on off."

"Well, no . . . I guess I wouldn't miss whatever is going to happen next," Doc said.

At that he pulled his pistol, so as to make sure it was loaded.

·50·

"I've a notion to hang you here and now, Earp," Old Man Clanton said. Spitting as he spoke.

"I'm sure you'd enjoy it, but I doubt you've got the manpower," Wyatt said. "And for my part I'd like to find a good bathtub and give you a solid scrubbing. You're about the dirtiest specimen I've seen this year."

Indeed, the old man was filthy to an extreme degree. Not only did he dip a lot of snuff; he also seemed to spill most of what he ate on himself.

"Why'd you stop my ox, you dirty scoundrel?" Old Man Clanton asked.

"It wasn't so much Monte," Wyatt said. "I kind of like Monte. In fact if you get tired of the expense we'd be happy to keep Monte as a pet. What we can't have is your damn cattle trampling through the main street of Tombstone—it throws up dust and scares the chickens. Cattle herds are illegal in Tombstone now."

Doc was startled by the last statement, since trail herds had been passing through pretty regularly since he had come there. Probably Wyatt was just running some kind of bluff, one that would provoke Old Man Clanton—if that was his aim he succeeded.

"The hell you say," the old man said, "I'll drive my damn cattle anywhere I want to take them."

"Nope, not anymore you can't," Wyatt informed him.

"Who's going to stop me?" Clanton asked.

"Why, me and the boys and maybe Doc here," Wyatt said. He pointed to the roof, where three of his brothers sat with rifles ready.

Meanwhile the riders to the south did not seem to be coming any closer.

"I'll bring hell down upon you, you smug son of a bitch. I'll go home and round up forty riders, and I'll drive my cattle anywhere I please, and one place I please is Tombstone."

"Just try it and we'll see that you're the first to die," Wyatt said.

The filthy old man did seem to be unarmed, but both Wyatt and Doc kept a close eye on him anyway. Their suspicions were justified, because Old Man Clanton rummaged in a saddlebag and came out with a heavy pistol.

Wyatt leveled his own pistol.

"Be careful with that hogleg," he said, calmly.

"It's not your time, Earp," the old man said. "But your time ain't long from now."

He rode over to where Monte was calmly chewing his cud, put his pistol an inch from the oxen's forehead, and fired three times. Like a great boat sinking, Monte the red ox sank to the ground, dead.

"Hell, you just killed your own best animal," Doc said. "Why?"

His shock was genuine.

"He worked for me, not you," Clanton said.

"I doubt Monte thought of it that way," Wyatt said.

Old Man Clanton whistled to his vaqueros and the whole mass of cattle began to move.

Unsoothed by Monte or any of the horrific vaqueros, the mass of animals began to move, but not through the main street of Tombstone. They stampeded and scattered wildly. By dawn most of the vaqueros had given up. No serious effort to round them up was ever made. Many went east into New Mexico; for years the Animas region swarmed with unclaimed cattle. A popular dime novelist wrote a dime novel called *Ghost Herd of the Animas*. It sold a million copies. Forty years later tourists thought they saw ghost cattle racing through the sage at dawn. Wyatt and Doc were often mentioned, and yet neither of them had fired a shot.

·51·

When Ike Clanton heard his father's report on the incident in Tombstone he threw his hat to the ground in disgust and then stomped on it, watched by his father and his popular curly-headed brother Billy Clanton. Billy was the only Clanton to be liked by all.

Ike was less popular, both within the family and out: to say that he had a temper would be to understate.

"Monte's been like a pet to me my whole life," Ike said.

"Get a new pet," Old Man Clanton said. "The damn ox turned aside when he was supposed to keep the herd on the move."

The McLaury brothers, Frank and Tom, were watching Ike's outburst with amusement. They had seen Ike fly off the handle before, and so had Curly Bob Brocius. Johnny Ringo was in the neighborhood but preferred to make his own camp.

"Now that you've ruined a good hat, go hobble the horses," Old Man Clanton told him.

"Billy can do that," Ike protested. He was about to protest further when a look in his father's eye caused him to back off. When his look got in a shooting mood he was apt to shoot just about anything.

"Maybe I'll go kill the whole passel of them Earps, inasmuch as they're a curse upon the land," the old man said. "We were supposed to deliver that herd of cattle to the railroad station in Animas in four days' time, and thanks to the Earps we barely have half a herd."

"Okay, I'll kill Wyatt, it won't take but a minute," Ike said.

His father looked at him scornfully.

"I'm sorry I bothered to sire a person as dumb as you," he said.

Just then a rifle shot rang out and Old Man Clanton pitched forward into the campfire. Curly Bob and a vaquero pulled him out, but the rifle shots kept firing. The horses whinnied—since Ike had not yet hobbled them most of them ran off. Curly Bob felt it expedient to roll under the chuck wagon. The McLaury brothers hid behind some yucca. Billy, no stranger to violence, fired his guns wildly. No one shot him.

When the shooting stopped four people were dead: Old Man Clanton, two vaqueros, and a cowboy named Bill.

No pursuit was attempted, and no one was ever charged.

·52·

Goodnight received the news of Old Man Clanton's death by letter while in Las Cruces, New Mexico, where he had delivered a sizable herd. Normally when on the trail he slept with the cowboys, but since selling large numbers of livestock usually meant dealing with a banker, he had spent the night in a hotel, just west of the Rio Grande.

"Nellie Courtright," he muttered; it was her handwriting on the envelope. There was merely a brief clipping from a newspaper in Albuquerque. It read:

> Newman Haynes Clanton, prominent Arizona rancher, with vast holdings near the border, was killed yesterday by assailant or assailants unknown. It is thought that the killers fled to Mexico, leaving a large herd of cattle mainly dispersed . . .

There was also a note from Nellie telling him to come see her
and bring his lady. Goodnight handed the note to Bose, who
had recently learned to read; in Mary Goodnight's school, no
less. Now he could read almost as good as his boss.

"He was a mean old man," Bose said.

"Yes he was," Goodnight said. "But for luck I might have
killed him myself."

They were waiting for the bank to open and Goodnight's
impatience was beginning to get the better of him.

"No more work than you have to do in a day it's a damn
nuisance when you don't show up to do it," he told the banker,
when the man finally arrived. Bose, who often carried money
from one bank to another, found bankers not to be very punc-
tual people, but he himself didn't care, whereas his boss did.
One thing that could be said about Charles Goodnight is that
he did not like to waste time.

·53·

"I know damn well Wyatt killed that old man—don't you agree?" Doc said to Jessie, who was making very good money due to the general prosperity Tombstone was enjoying. She was as curious as Doc about Wyatt's movements during the time of the killing of Old Man Clanton, but she knew Wyatt better than Doc did and could not say positively that Wyatt or somebody hired had killed the old rustler.

When Wyatt came back into the saloon after four days gone and she asked where he had been he merely frowned at her and didn't answer. He then spent the next few days in a rival saloon, not the Last Kind Words. It was nearly a week before he kissed her, making it difficult to be a wife to him. Sometimes she didn't even know why she tried.

For his part Doc was having trouble getting much out of Wyatt.

"You ain't invisible, you know, Wyatt," Doc said.

"I never claimed invisibility, though I am sly," Wyatt said. He knew that Doc and most of the rest of Arizona were still worrying the mystery of who killed Old Man Clanton, a mystery about which Wyatt himself had nothing to say. Predictions of a feud between the Earps and the Clantons were rife. Most of the citizens of Cochise County were loaded down with firearms now—though neither the Clantons nor the Earps had verifiably done anything violent—unless you count Ike Clanton stomping on his hat.

"If you went all the way into New Mexico to kill that old bastard, then somebody probably saw you," Doc said.

"If that's your opinion, publish it in the damn paper for all I care," Wyatt countered.

"I rarely read the paper," he went on. "Nothing they publish is likely to disturb my sleep."

"I do regret Monte, though," he added. "I liked that damn ox."

"Still, it wouldn't hurt you to tell me where you've been for four days," Doc said.

"I will point out that four days ain't long," Wyatt said. "I could have just been up the street, drinking rye whiskey for four days."

"You can be an aggravating cuss," Doc mentioned. "Of course none of the Clantons except young Billy is exactly popular either," Doc admitted.

At least the law locally was in the hands of the two gentler Earps, Virgil and Morgan. They weren't soft men by any means, but they were't hard like Wyatt.

Meanwhile, most days, Doc was spitting blood.

·54·

The violent death of Newman Haynes Clanton caused an immediate reshuffling of power in the rustling crowd. The Clantons were determined to hold on to their part of the border: the part where it was easiest to funnel their Mexican cattle through. The McLaurys threw in with the Clantons, at least for a time. Both groups tried to get Johnny Ringo to ride with them, but he declined to participate. Besides cards his main interest was a young whore named Sally, who lived in a hut behind the Last Kind Words Saloon.

It was said that Newton Earp also loved the little whore, but little was known about Newton Earp, the shiest of the Earp boys, probably.

The joker in the local deck, so Wyatt believed, was the lanky pistolero who called himself Johnny-Behind-the-Deuce, who was said to be the best in the West—or anywhere—at throwing rocks.

"They say he can knock quails out of the air with a rock—I doubt that, myself," Doc said.

Wyatt, who had been gloomy, perked up suddenly at the thought of a rock-throwing competition. He promptly marched right into the saloon and introduced himself to the rock thrower.

"You don't have to say my whole name," Johnny said. "I worked a medecine show once and they gave me this long name and it stuck."

"So which part of it are we supposed to use?" Wyatt asked.

"Just call me Deuce," the stranger said. "I despise a long-winded name."

When asked if he could knock quail out of the air with rocks, the newcomer looked surprised that anyone would care.

"Where I come from, which is Scotland, it's a common skill," he explained.

"Mister, this ain't Scotland," Wyatt said, and proceeded to lay bets on the outcome. Fortunately quail were plentiful in the outskirts of Tombstone. The Mexican cook at the Last Kind Words Saloon kept a pen full for customers who grew tired of beefsteak.

The stranger who allowed himself to be called Deuce warmed up by knocking over a few bottles Wyatt had sat on a wall. Wyatt was openly scornful of the proceedings. Johnny Deuce, as Doc preferred to call him, asked Wyatt to release the bobwhites one at a time, whereas the pretty Gambrils quail preferred to run between the chaparral bushes.

To Wyatt's astonishment, Doc's, and the the local spectators, the lanky Scot coolly knocked over his first ten quail, six flying and four on the ground.

"No fair, you didn't turn them loose high enough," Wyatt said to Doc, who had been releasing the quail.

"Wyatt, there ain't no right way to start up a dang quail," Doc said.

"Hell, I never supposed he'd be this good," Wyatt said.

"Hell yourself, I never even heard of throwing rocks at quail," Doc admitted.

The Scotsman kept throwing and quail kept falling. Wyatt, who was notoriously hard to impress about anything, was openmouthed with astonishment at what he was seeing.

"Dern, it's worth losing a hundred dollars to witness skill like that," he said,

Johnny Deuce just shrugged.

"My pa once hit one hundred and two," he said. "The only reason he had to quit then was because he ran out of rocks."

"Well, there's no danger of that here," Wyatt said, looking around at the rocky hills. "No danger at all."

·55·

Wyatt and Doc were taking their ease on the porch of the Last Kind Words Saloon when a little procession rode by, trying to look dangerous. There was Ike and Billy Clanton, two McLaurys, several cowboys, and a few vaqueros. It was a quiet day in Tombstone. Johnny Ringo had left town on business, and the rock-throwing Scot had loped off toward Tucson.

"I thought those Clantons ran a cattle ranch," Wyatt said. "Why don't they work a little instead of cluttering the streets and making damn nuisances of themselves."

"It's mainly Ike that's the nuisance," Doc said. "The others will probably just get drunk and play cards."

"I might be of a different opinion," Wyatt said.

But he seemed inclined to let the matter drop, and probably would have had not Ike Clanton, the principal nuisance, come swaggering down the street with a gun in his hand, though it wasn't pointed at anyone.

"Get out of that chair and face me," Ike, who was short, said. "You son of a bitch," he added, as a kind of flourish.

Wyatt and Doc looked at one another.

"Which son of a bitch did you want to fight, Ike?" Doc inquired politely.

"Hell, I don't know," Ike admitted. "You've both got a licking coming, though I could save time and shoot you."

Wyatt stood up and lazily walked over to Ike, who was clearly drunk.

"I'm afraid your eyes have got bigger than your stomach, Ike," Wyatt said. "You could no more whip me than you can fly."

"Nor could you whip me, you young fool," Doc said.

It was then that the confusion began for Ike Clanton, who had not yet bothered to cock his weapon. Wyatt Earp, who had just been sitting on the porch paring his nails, suddenly got behind him with a rifle, that he used to whack Ike in the head. Ike suddenly saw the ground come up and meet his head, hard.

"I'll take your weapon, it's for your own good," Wyatt told him. He waved at his brother Morgan, who was a block away, awaiting developments.

"He's a rowdy one," he said, handing his rifle and Ike's pistol to Doc. Then he took Ike by his pants leg and began to drag him over to Morgan, who was acting as the jailer.

"Why didn't you just shoot him?" Morgan asked.

"No, no . . . it's too early in the day for gunplay," Wyatt said. "Jail him until he sobers up and then insist that he leave town and take his damn friends with him. And keep the pistol."

Ike Clanton had his eyes open, but did not immediately have anything to say.

"It's fine for you to be whacking people with your Winchester, Wyatt, but there are practical aspects to jailing people, one being that the jail's full. Some of those gamblers we arrested last night ain't woke up yet."

Wyatt smiled. Morgan often got himself into practical difficulties. He had been a studious child too.

"It could be that you need a bigger jail, too," Wyatt said. "If you don't have a cell free, just chain Ike to an anvil or something. Don't let him go until he's full sober."

With that he walked off. Ike was just beginning to stir. His head had a sizable lump on it.

At the last minute Wyatt decided to keep Ike's pistol himself, though it was a poor weapon, of dubious accuracy.

"I venture to guess that you've made an enemy," Doc said.

"No, he was already my enemy," Wyatt said. "I thought best to disarm him."

Doc stood up and assessed the situation. Billy Clanton came down the street and was trying to talk Morgan Earp out of his prisoner. Perhaps because of the overcrowded jail; or because Morgan often refused to do what Wyatt said, Billy was soon leading an unstable Ike back up the street toward the O.K. Corral, where the Clantons and the McLaurys had their horses stabled.

"I guess Morgan can't tolerate a messy jail," Doc said, to Wyatt, who shrugged. "He should have picked somebody besides Ike to turn loose. Ike's a hothead."

Wyatt looked up the street and saw that the McLaurys and a few of their hired hands had taken an interest in the proceedings.

"If Ike goes home I'll let him be, but if he makes trouble I'll give him a lick he won't forget," Wyatt said.

"Unless he shoots you," Doc said.

"He won't, I took his gun."

"Wyatt, wake up," Doc said. "There's more guns in this town than there are birds in the sky. It won't take Ike more than ten minutes to rearm."

Wyatt knew that was true. But he didn't feel worried. Ike Clanton was a fool and a loudmouth, but not a killer. In his view Ike would avoid conflict, though that didn't mean the McLaurys would.

"Wyatt, are you a damn marshal now?" Doc asked. "If you're not, what business do you have arresting people?"

"Oh, I didn't actually *arrest* Ike," Wyatt said. "I left the arresting to Morgan and Virg."

Doc let it drop, though he had an uneasy feeling. If Wyatt was already in an arresting mood, who could say what might happen later in the day.

He himself was unarmed at the time, but Wells Fargo was only a block away, and they always had a gun or two that they were willing to lend to sober citizens like himself. A shotgun might be best; it would only be prudent. Wyatt had a kind of crazy look in his eye—it might be well to be armed.

When he stood up to go inquire about the shotgun, Wyatt Earp was standing in the street; he was still watching the small crowd gathered at the O.K. Corral.

·56·

Jessie happened to be looking out her window when Wyatt walked out to deal with Ike Clanton—she was brushing her teeth and getting ready to comb her hair. Wyatt was moving slow, smiling at Ike in a friendly way; but then suddenly he stepped to his right and whacked Ike with the barrel of the rifle he was carrying.

Ike fell face forward into the dusty street and didn't move for a while. Wyatt took Ike's pistol away from him and gave it to Morgan, who slipped it into his coat pocket.

Wyatt and Morgan chatted a minute, and then Wyatt walked back over to where Doc Holliday waited. Doc appeared to be unarmed.

Jessie had slept badly, and Wyatt too. Now and then through the night, he put his hand on her, but that was as far as matters went. Jessie hoped it would go farther; after all, she was awake and there they were. But Wyatt didn't do much and she didn't dare make an overture herself; he would just go icy, and it might be days before he was friendly again.

"You married one of the most difficult men on the planet, Jessie," Doc told her once. "You should have married an old pussycat like me."

"Oh yeah," Jessie said. "Then why did Katie Elder tell me you've broken her nose twice?"

She said it mainly just to keep a conversation going. Katie Elder, though a friend, was not always to be believed.

"Ha, that liar," Doc said. "She's got the biggest nose in the Territory anyway."

"If I was to hit her I imagine I'd break my hand," he said a little later.

For her part Jessie considered Doc to be the biggest liar in the Territory, but at least he was friendly and her husband wasn't.

·57·

Frank McLaury was for going home. It was certainly rude of the Earps to act as if they owned the town of Tombstone. True, the town had made Virgil Earp sheriff and his brother Morgan deputy, but, so far as Frank knew, they hadn't made Wyatt anything and Wyatt was the one causing all the trouble. There he was, fifty yards down the street, looking at them as if they were the worst outlaws in the Territory, when in fact they were just harmless cattlemen, come to town for a little gambling and a visit to the bank.

"Look at him," Frank said. "You'd think he was the governor or something."

"Besides that he killed Pa. I'd bet a hundred dollars it was him," Ike said. He was still groggy and so far had failed to obtain a new gun. He had lost most of his cash earlier in the day, in a poker game, and would have to borrow from his little brother Billy, or else from one of the McLaurys; but they were known to be a frugal pair, not likely to be sympathetic to his plight.

A photographer had set up a little studio next door to the O.K. Corral, but the man was a newcomer and could not be expected to lend a weapon on such short notice.

He wondered what the odds were that Wyatt would have mellowed to the point where he would simply give him his gun back; he decided the odds were slim.

"I say we just go home—there'll be a better day," Frank McLaury repeated. "The Earps have got their dander up, for some damn reason," he continued. "What do you think, Billy?"

Billy Clanton, the youngest person there, had no firm opinion.

"Don't care," Billy said. "I'm too young to be let in the saloons, and there ain't much for me to do."

"I guess you could play mumbly-peg with Indian Charlie, if you can find him," Frank McLaury suggested.

"No thanks, I don't think I've sunk that low."

In fact Billy had his eye on the whore named Sally Whistle, but Sally worked for money and he didn't have any. All avenues of enjoyment at the moment seemed out of reach.

Tom McLaury was the most combative member of his family, and he was up for a fight.

"No Earp, nor party of Earps, is going to run me out of Tombstone," he declared.

"Okay then, let's take a walk and maybe the Earps will just forget about us," Ike suggested.

"Walk? Where in hell would you want to walk, in Tombstone?" Tom asked.

"Just around," Ike said. He didn't expect his idea to be welcomed. His brothers were so unused to walking that they would mount a horse just to walk across a pen or corral.

To his surprise the McLaurys and his brother Billy suddenly ambled off toward the photographer's shop, smoking cheroots as they went.

"Hey, we could get our pictures taken," he said.

"No, I've not got time for such frivolity," Frank McLaury said. "I'll saunter over to the depot and back, and hope the Earps will break a leg, or do something, by the time we get back."

"And I still say we ought to be sensible and just go home," he added. It might be a long wait before the quarrelsome Earps got in a better mood.

"Heck no, I'm in a fine mood myself," Tom said. "If the Earps know what's good for them they'll leave me be."

At that point Ike gave up.

·58·

"There's laws against mobs assembling in this town," Wyatt insisted. "And if there ain't I'll make one up myself."

"You're afflicted with the means today, Wyatt," Doc informed him.

Just then two ore wagons went blazing through town, covering the whole area with dust—for a moment it was difficult to see even as far as the O.K. Corral.

"Ike and Billy and Frank and Tom," Doc counted. "Four ignorant cowboys don't make a mob. And anyway Billy Clanton is too young to count."

"What about Indian Charlie—he's lurking around," Wyatt said.

"I have no quarrel with Indian Charlie," Virgil mentioned.

"I guess you boys are forgiving of sinners," Wyatt said. "I

say we go run a bluff on them and chase them out of town, so the sight of them won't be so damn aggravating."

"Hold on, I'll just go borrow that shotgun from Wells Fargo," Doc said. "Better to have it and not need it than need it and not have it. That's a sentiment I wouldn't mind having on my gravestone, if I'm lucky enough to have a gravestone."

"Do you really want to do this, Wyatt?" he asked. "I don't see the necessity, myself."

"It's just a bluff, Doc . . . no shooting unless we really have to."

His own weapon, at the moment, was the sorry pistol that had once been Ike Clanton's. He had got it back from Morgan.

Doc quickly borrowed a serviceable .12 gauge. Morgan and Virg, professional lawmen both, each had Colts.

When they headed up the dusty street, Virgil took the left side, Morgan the right, with Wyatt and Doc in the middle. Two more ore wagons came through and an abundance of dust lingered.

To their surprise, when they got within bluffing distance of the O.K. Corral, neither Clantons nor McLaurys were in sight.

"The damn scamps, where'd they go?" Wyatt asked.

"Probably gave it up and left," Doc said.

"Maybe they're smarter than I gave them credit for," Wyatt said.

Indian Charlie appeared suddenly, causing everyone to jump, but he was merely raking up horse turds from the livery stable.

"This is a damn waste of time," Wyatt said.

"Now didn't I predict that very thing?" Doc said. "I told you to leave it be."

But just as he said it gunfire erupted and Morgan went down.
"No, no . . . I don't want this," Virgil said. "I'm the sheriff."
Then he went down too.

Ike Clanton quickly ran into the photographer's shop and was not shot. Both McLaurys fired and Wyatt killed them both. Somebody hit young Billy Clanton, who died after a brief agony.

Doc was nicked, Wyatt untouched. A wagon had to be brought to bring Morgan and Virgil to the doctor.

When Wyatt walked in on Jessie she grabbed him and held him tight and kissed him passionately.

"You fool, you could have been killed," Jessie said, crying.

"Yes, but I wasn't; let go," Wyatt said.

NELLIE'S VISITS

by Nellie Courtright

ONCE I GOT BITTEN by the journalism bug there was nothing to stop me from going wherever the stories took me, which was pretty much all over our Old West as it was waning. I often saw the Goodnights—or at least Charlie; his Mary had died. Sturdy as she seemed, the panhandle of Texas was just no place for a lady—not then. The plow had never touched the range country, not then.

The first time I visited Charlie after Mary's death we sat out on the porch until late at night, not talking much, just watching the stars come out. I lived in Santa Monica then, a block from the Pacific, which didn't allow for many stars.

"I'm an old bachelor and it don't suit me," Charlie said. "I'd be mighty pleased if you'd marry me."

I was so surprised I almost fainted—then I remembered that I had kissed him once.

"I'm flattered, Charlie," I said. "But as far as I know I'm still married to Zenas."

"How long has he been gone?" he asked.

"About eighteen years," I said.

Charlie gave a kind of snort.

"You don't have a husband, you just have an excuse," he said. "I'll throw in a hundred head of cattle, to sweeten the offer," he said.

"Charlie, I'm a city girl," I said. "I wouldn't know what to do with myself out here on the baldies."

"That's that, then," he said. "Good night."

Some years later I heard he married his nurse and I also heard that he got swindled out of most of his land. He might have been a great man, Charlie—I'm glad I kissed him and also glad I didn't marry him—I saw enough of the prairie during my years in Rita Blanca.

I had long forgotten Wyatt Earp and his violent brothers when he was brought to my attention by a story in a newspaper about a riot that took place in Oakland. There had been a big prizefight and Wyatt Earp had been the referee. Wyatt awarded the fight to a man named Sharkey and the crowd didn't like the verdict and rioted for a while, though Wyatt himself escaped unharmed.

The piece mentioned that Wyatt lived in San Pedro, just down the beach a ways. I found him in the phone book and called him up and got Jessie—I don't think she really remembered me but she invited me to drop by anyway. I had a little rolltop convertible then, so I put the top down and went briskly down to San Pedro.

I had barely arrived before I wished I hadn't. Wyatt and Jessie lived in a dilapidated little bungalow. Their yard was filled with junk: old tires, some buckets, a saddle, tools of various kinds, a wheelbarrow, and the like.

Wyatt was sitting on the porch in an old wicker chair he had found someplace. I don't think he really recognized me, but Jessie sort of did. She had always been a large woman, but now she had spread, while Wyatt seemed to have shrunk. The famous hero of the O.K. Corral was now a rheumy-eyed old man who spent his days spitting tobacco into a coffee can.

"No point in asking him about the killing," Jessie said. "Wyatt don't remember much—there's days when he barely remembers me."

Then she tried to introduce us—sunken as she was, she had some trace of manners.

"Wyatt, we used to know this lady," she said. "We knew her in Long Grass. She wrote for the newspaper."

Wyatt looked at me but I'm not sure he saw me.

"Did you know Doc?" he asked. "Doc died of the TB, up in Colorado."

"I'm sorry to hear about it—I didn't know him well."

By then I was sorry I had come. There was nothing

to be had from the Earps, and their sorrow was making me sad. Jessie did tell me that Wyatt had taught Sunday school, at a big church up on Wilshire.

As I was picking my way through the junk in the yard I saw something I had all but forgotten: Warren Earp's Last Kind Words Saloon sign, lying on top of some tires. There it was in San Pedro, far from Long Grass, where I first saw it.

"Jessie, can I buy this sign? I remember it from Long Grass."

Jessie seemed puzzled, that anyone would want such a thing.

"Just take it, honey—we got no use for it," she said. "Warren Earp drug it around all over the place. We never did know what he meant by it."

"How is Warren?" I asked, to be polite.

Jesse looked at me in surprise, as if I had forgotten something I was supposed to know.

"Dead," she said. "Dead a long time ago."

So I took the sign, not quite sure why I wanted it, put it in the back of my convertible, and drove away.

The End

PHOTO CREDITS

ABOUT THE AUTHOR

LARRY MCMURTRY is the author of thirty novels, including the Pulitzer Prize–winning *Lonesome Dove*. His other works include three essay collections, five memoirs, and more than forty screenplays, including the coauthorship (with Diana Ossana) of *Brokeback Mountain*, for which he received an Academy Award. He lives in Archer City, Texas.